Fikret Pajalic

Complication

SHORT STORIES

First Published in 2023 by Pishukin Press

http://www.pishukinpress.com/

Copyright © 2023 by Fikret Pajalic

Cover design: Created using Canva elements, Photo 13281756 © Vvoronov | Dreamstime.com

Pre-publication data is available from the National Library of Australia trove.nla.gov.au

Paperback edition: ISBN 9781922871336

Complication
SHORT STORIES

Content Warnings

SCAN QR CODE

OR GO TO

www.fikretpajalic.com/
themes.html

Contents

BOONIE

A couple of weeks after I started my new job, a woman from the office took a shine to me. Her name was Wanda and she was the payroll lady. She had some Polish blood in her somewhere along the line and she understood a few words of my language. She had a nice, round, pleasant Slavic face. I liked faces like that.

This happened right after I went to live with my mate in his old weatherboard house in Tottenham, close to the train station. Train wheels screeched in my ears during the night, keeping me from sleep.

I got the warehouse job where Wanda worked because my mate quit. He was a truckie and he wanted to go and work up north, try mining, so I ended up minding his house. I didn't have to pay rent, just utilities, and I had to take care of his dog Max.

'When I settle in, I'll come and get Max,' my mate said.

Max chewed on an old cricket bat and glared at me.

I wasn't keen on being a dog sitter. I could keep an eye on the house, all right. The house didn't move.

'Max is old,' my mate said, 'he doesn't need much these days.'

We shook hands. Before he left, he said he'd dropped my name with his ex-boss. So I went to this place on Sunshine Road where they used to make work pants and shirts, but now it was just a warehouse where all sorts of stuff from China arrived. Everything from picture frames to garden furniture.

I got a job as a forklift driver. It was a small operation. There were a dozen or so of us in the warehouse, our boss and two ladies up in the office.

I filled out the paperwork, and Wanda took me to the warehouse. When the boss introduced me to the blokes, he struggled to say my name properly.

He said, 'Sorry mate, I can't bloody say it.'

I was going to say my name slowly and loudly to the group, I'm used to this shit, when some fatso with a face that looked like a bag of walnuts said, 'We'll call you Frank.'

The boss looked at me and said, 'Is that all right, mate? It's kind of similar sounding.'

I needed the job, so I nodded. Wanda's lips formed into a line that stretched her round cheeks. After the introduction, she asked me to follow her, saying my name as my mother would. She issued me with steel-capped boots, a uniform and a forklift key.

After I gave her my signature, she put her hand on my shoulder and with a smile said, 'Good luck.'

I smiled back.

By the end of the day, I was Frank. One old codger called me Franklin. No one knew my real name.

As I was leaving work that day, Walnut Face stopped his green Falcon near me, wound down the window and said, 'Mate, you can't expect us to remember that mouthful every time we call you.' He spat at my feet and drove off.

I sat in my car and looked at the warehouse. Wanda was in the window looking at me. She waved before I drove off, and I did the same.

Wanda was forty plus, blonde hair in a bun, great figure, big matronly boobs halfway down her waist. She'd come down to the warehouse and offer guys overtime or weekend shifts. She'd always come to me first. When I had my lunch on the benches outside, she'd come down with some sandwiches or something she cooked the night before. Soon I didn't bother bringing food.

One day she said, 'I've got these varicose veins and they're hurting a lot.' She put on that damsel in distress voice and it got me going.

She pulled her skirt above her knees and I saw little purple rivers running from her feet all the way up to her thighs. I offered to massage her feet. I said some bullshit story about how a few years back I completed half a course in physiotherapy at St Albans TAFE. I also said I had strong hands. I pumped up my biceps and she giggled as she touched them. She said she might take me up on the massage.

'You could walk to my place. I'm only two streets away,' she said.

I said I might do that.

Then she launched into her life problems. She told me she was married to a chap who liked to stick his nose into everything. His name was Brad. The first time we did it in her car, I had to listen to her talk about Brad for half an hour. Then we did it. She had a Camry station wagon and when we dropped the seats there was heaps of room for a romp. We fucked in the parking lot after everyone had gone home. For a lady her age she could go the distance and was a great root, but as soon as we stopped fucking, she talked about her husband. She said the last time her mother visited, while they were eating Sunday roast, her husband asked her mum at what age she started her period.

'This was right in front of my son, Richie. Richie's twelve, for fuck's sake!' Wanda said.

I saw Richie once when I gave Wanda a ride home. He worked on his bike in the front yard. He was blonde and blue eyed, just like his mother, and there were dark blue marks on his neck and scabs on his forearms.

I kept seeing Wanda even after her husband started coming to work and threatening every bloke that if he found out who was fucking his wife, he'd kill him. Wanda would come down to calm him and he'd cry and beg her to stop whoring herself.

Wanda didn't listen. She left him and went back to her mother's house in Deer Park, taking her boy with her. We didn't see each other for a couple of weeks and when we met again, she said her weakling husband had lost the plot.

'Couldn't give me some space, wouldn't take his meds.'

She said he found her in the shopping centre and gave her two days to come to her senses. When Wanda didn't, he came with a couple of his mates to her mother's house and they went berserk. They smashed her place up, wrote off all the walls. Her husband cut the furniture with a knife and then tried to kill himself in the lounge room. After that, the cops came.

'Now he's locked up and on watch,' Wanda said.

I felt there was more to the whole thing, but didn't ask her any questions. I just sat on the sofa next to her and gently touched her hand or knee. I'd make her coffee and something to eat. Every now and then I'd say something like 'I understand' or 'that's not on'.

She'd say things like 'you're so good to me' and 'I can't believe you don't have a girlfriend'. I told her my wife left me and she gasped. After she'd had a good rant about her husband, we'd root. She'd always get horny after trash-mouthing him.

We kept up with seeing each other. I started working like crazy. My bones hurt. I wanted to save for a house deposit. I worked hard all week and at night I'd have a few drinks to relax. On telly, the new crop of Aussie batsmen was putting a high price on their wickets just like David Boon once did. Then sometimes I'd have a few cones just to wind down and go to sleep so I could get up the next day and put in a twelve or fourteen hour shift.

After I forgot to feed Max a few times, I bought a second-hand dog self-feeder off the internet. It cost me thirty bucks.

I was driving back from work when I saw Max running on the paddock next to the train station. Some boys on their bikes were riding in a circle and Max was running with them. I parked the car and whistled. Max stopped running and looked my way. I whistled again, and the boys stopped riding. Max turned his head toward them. One of the boys on a blue mountain bike dismounted and went to his knees. He patted Max on his neck and head and then pointed toward me. He waved at me. I squinted to see better. It was Richie.

I called, 'Over here, Max,' and Max licked Richie's face before trotting my way. I couldn't figure out how he'd jumped the fence. When I got home, I looked to see if he'd dug a hole under it.

The next morning at work, I told Wanda about it. 'The last thing I need is to lose my mate's dog.'

She asked what type of dog Max was, and I said I wasn't sure.

'He looks like that dog from the first Mad Max movie. He's got a patch on his right eye and a thick grey-blue coat.'

Wanda laughed. 'You're having me on, aren't you?' she asked.

'I'm not. He looks like a pirate, I'm telling you.' I crossed my heart.

'I can't believe you don't know that's a heeler. He's a cattle dog. They jump on cows' backs to round them up. That's your answer.'

'But he's old. A grandfather, really.'

'Doesn't matter. He must be bored.'

That day, I came back home from work and I found Max tied to one of the porch railings. The rope was short, and it was tied tight around his neck so he couldn't sit. His tail was tucked between his legs. When he saw me, he barked in relief. His bark was weak and coarse. He shivered when I untied him and leaped into my embrace. As I stroked his back, I felt a cold, oily dampness between my fingers and the smell of petrol hit my nostrils.

I found a piece of paper stapled to the front door. There was no message on it. A single matchstick was taped to the paper.

I looked up and down the empty street. Nothing moved. Even the tree branches were still. I couldn't hear any birds. Rain started to spit.

I took Max inside and washed him in the bathtub. He didn't protest. He stayed still, happy to be clean again. I dried him and placed a bowl of food and bowl of water in the hallway. Max dug into his biscuits.

In the kitchen, I turned on the stovetop and filled a small pot with water and put it to boil. I was going to make macaroni cheese for myself. I was serious about saving money. As the water slowly came to the boil, my anger rose with it.

Max stopped eating and ran to the front door. He made a low growl. I heard people talking outside. I peered through the curtains and saw four men on the footpath. The afternoon was growing dark from the rain.

One of the men grabbed his own forearm, opened his mouth wide and started biting the air, making a crazy face. His eyes rolled up until there were only whites visible. The fat one joined this performance and checked the hand of the crazy man, who now pretended to squirm in pain. Bastards knew they were being watched. I had a better look at the fat one. It was Walnut Face from work. Further down the street, I could see his green Falcon, a bike sticking out of the boot. A blonde head poked out of the backseat window. Max jumped on the windowsill and when he saw Richie's head in the car, he barked and wagged his tail. He turned to me with his pleading eyes and whined.

The men talked some more and then one of them walked to my front door. The bell rang. I went to the kitchen and turned off the hotplate before I opened the front door.

The man said, 'I'm Brad from down the street. Can I talk to you for a moment, mate?'

Wanda's ex had bulging eyes and flaky skin. He rubbed his right palm with the thumb of his left hand like he was hurt.

I said, 'What's this about?'

'You're Frank, right?' His eyes darted back to the street where the other three men stood watching.

'I'm not,' I said.

'You're not?'

'No.'

'You're not what?' Brad asked, confused.

'I'm not Frank.'

'I was told that was your name.'

'Who told you that?' I peered over his shoulder.

'The neighbours,' he said and looked at the street again.

I pulled out my wallet and showed him my driver's licence. Brad leaned in and squinted.

'But how do you say it?'

I stayed quiet and stared into Brad's eyes. They were red, no glint in them. Lack of sleep, maybe.

'I heard that's your name. All right if I call you Frank? I'll call you Frank, all right. In any case, that's not why I'm here.'

Brad turned to his buddies.

I looked up and down the street. It was lined with saplings along the footpaths. There were houses with bright red roofs and inside them were people like Brad and his three mates and their wives. Some had children, some had cats and others had dogs. A train whistled in the distance.

'Get to the point,' I said to Brad.

Brad said Max had chased his son who was riding his bike and that his son had fallen and broken his leg. He said his son smashed into a rock somewhere in the paddock near the station when he fell, and it was Max's fault.

I knew the land around the station well. It was flat, nothing on it. There were no rocks or trees or anything. Just flat, muddy earth.

'Any witnesses to this?' I asked.

'My son doesn't lie.' Brad stiffened. 'Your dog's a heeler. Heelers chase.'

'I've never seen Max run out to the paddock,' I lied.

'You haven't been looking, then,' Brad snorted. He put a cigarette in his mouth and lit it.

'What do you want, Brett?'

'It's Brad.' He took a deep drag on his cigarette. 'I'll tell you what I came for.'

'Hang on, Brett. I've got something on the stove. Be right back.'

I returned with the note and its matchstick. I shoved it in Brad's chest and told him to read it. Then I reached for the cricket bat behind the door and leaned on it like the once impenetrable David Boon. Max sat next to me and growled. Brad looked at the note, then at Max, and stepped back. I lifted the bat in the air and took a stand as if I was facing a delivery. Then I pretended to play pull shot. I swung the bat above Brad's head, the willow swooshed, and he ducked.

'The Tassie boys,' I said, 'they could play pull shot like no one else.'

'What?' Brad said.

'You know. Ponting and Boon. You follow cricket?'

'Not here to talk sports, mate,' Brad said.

'I reckon it's time for you to take a walk. Think of it as a Yorker right on the shins.' I tapped Brad's shins gently with the bat.

'All right, mate,' Brad stepped back and looked toward the car. I saw Richie slump in the seat under the weight of his father's stare and I started to feel sorry for him.

'Brad, mate,' I said, 'Listen. How about I take Max over to your son. Let them suss each other out. They'll be mates in no time.'

Brad and the rest of the men looked at me like they were staring at an abstract painting. Walnut Face clenched his fists. I still had the bat in my hand and Max by my side.

'That won't be necessary,' Brad said.

'I insist.' I walked out and passed the group of men. They pulled their collars high and their hats low to protect themselves from rain. I headed for the car.

Richie was crying in the back seat. He wiped his eyes with his shirtsleeve.

I looked at Richie's legs and there was nothing wrong with them. I opened the door and Max jumped into the boy's lap. They hugged. I walked to the back of the car and pulled the bike out. Richie followed Max out of the car and I told him to go home to his mother.

Max sat beside me, watching as Richie jumped on the bike and rode off. The dog snarled when Brad flicked his cigarette in my mate's front yard and the men started walking toward me. Night had arrived, and the rain was coming down harder. I couldn't hear the trains coming and going. The streetlights had all come on and the lamp above my head was buzzing. I put the bat between my legs and wiped my wet hands on my thighs. Max barked and barked. I gripped the bat and thought of the stocky batsman with a seriously thick moustache. He could really strike the ball.

THE FLOCK

Three weeks ago an envelope was jammed under the front door of Alma's flat. It was thick and the rubber sweep at the bottom of the screen door held it up. Alma, who was watching *Playschool* with her two children, a boy aged seven and a girl four, untangled herself from them and opened the door.

A young man hurriedly walked down the steps. Alma called after him. He stopped, half turned and made eye contact. She recognised him from the real estate agency. She paid her rent to him on many occasions, always cash, because that's how she got paid. Once, he told her she could set up a direct debit on her account so she didn't have to come to the office. She declined. Another time, he said he had a friend from Bosnia and asked her how to say some words in her language. He said he wanted to play a joke on him, make him laugh. She told him to look it up in a dictionary.

Alma lifted the letter up in the air.

'What's this?' She knew a letter jammed under the front door rarely brought good news.

The young man straightened his shoulders and wiped his eyebrows with his thumb. He introduced himself as Jonah. 'I didn't mean to disturb you,' he said, gesturing at the letter.

Alma repeated her question.

'It's your thirty-day termination notice,' the young man said, 'the flat is being sold.'

Alma looked at the thick letter, which had the real estate agent logo in the reddest red printed in the top left corner. She examined Jonah's face and noticed a flicker of something. Contrition?

She knew this could happen. She had a periodic tenancy agreement, which meant either party could end it at anytime.

'This is your notice, not mine,' she told him.

'I beg your pardon.'

'*You* are giving the notice to *me*.' She pointed at him and then at herself. 'This is your notice to me. *We* must leave the flat.' This time she pointed to the living room. 'Right?'

'Right, it's your notice —.'

'No, it can't be mine. I didn't write it. You wrote it. You typed it. You put it in the envelope. You brought it here and shoved it under my door. I never wanted it.'

'It's just an expression. A matter of speech, that's all. I'm sorry, lady.'

Alma looked at the flawless skin of the young man's face. She was only a few years older than him, but she had two children, no husband, and four years of war behind her. In his eyes, she was a lady. She'd lived in her new country long enough to know ladies were what older women were called here.

'Sorry for what?' Alma snarled. 'For the notice or for insulting my English?'

The young man opened his mouth but changed his mind. He started down the stairs.

'Why didn't you just post it or put in my letterbox?' Alma's question froze his foot midair, almost touching the step under it.

'I was in the vicinity. I thought this might give you a couple of extra days to look.' He put his foot on the step and waited for Alma to say something.

But she didn't. She saw the little ladybug cart toy on the landing. She'd borrowed it from the library for her daughter. She picked up the toy, turned on her heels, and closed the door. From the living room window, she watched him walk to a small motorcycle. Mopeds, they called them. Jonah mounted his moped, and she pulled back the curtain.

Why did they always introduce themselves? Alma wondered. She never asked his name and hated the fact she knew it. It's a tactic they employed. She was aware of this. With a name, he became a real, flesh and blood person, with his own problems and fears, not just some pencil pusher trained to deliver bad news to tenants. She disliked him regardless. She and her children had been tossed out on the street too many times for any other feelings to remain.

'What did he want?' her son came to stand beside her at the window.

Alma took him by the hand and sat him next to his sister.

'Let's all have some ice cream and I'll tell you about the adventure that awaits us.'

'Ice cream, yippee,' her daughter Azra screamed, 'I want vanilla. Vanilla!'

'Vanilla's all we have,' her brother Edin snapped.

A knock on the door interrupted Alma as she scooped ice cream into cones. She handed them to her children and returned to the front door.

Jonah launched into a monologue before she could say anything.

'The reason I came by is that you're legally entitled to sixty day notice. The tenancy law has been updated recently to accommodate people in hardship. The agency is giving you only thirty days, hoping you won't know this. I'm sorry. I should've been upfront with you. I was afraid if I said something to my boss, he'd sack me. I'm a student and need the job. I'm not from Melbourne either.'

'Thank you,' Alma stopped him before he completely embarrassed himself. 'Wait here.' She returned with an ice cream.

Jonah took the cone and said, 'I feel bad about this.'

'That's good,' Alma said.

'It is?'

'Feeling bad is sometimes good.'

Jonah stared at her, waiting for more, but all Alma said was goodbye and closed the door.

'I have good news,' she said to her children, with her bravest face on, 'we're leaving this flat. Mummy's going to find us a house.'

Alma's daughter screeched from joy, but her son remained quiet. He raised his eyebrows and Alma put her hands on his shoulders and kissed him on the forehead.

***

Alma tried to take care of her hands. Creams, lotions, protective gloves at work; she used it all with limited success. They were dry and cracked. The little bones didn't sit properly anymore, and she was in pain. But her arms were strong. Now she could lift and carry both of her children at the same time.

Alma worked as an on-call labourer in a chicken factory where she removed bones from thighs, skinned the whole chicken, cut it to pieces and anything else she was told, including emptying large square buckets full of chicken insides into the bowels of a truck from the pet food factory.

She also helped out in a kitchen at a cafe on Main Road West or stayed home looking after her two children when there was no work. When she did work, her children looked after each other. Their father, Alma's husband, never made it out of the Bosnian war. He was buried; she was told, in one of the mass graves that littered the Bosnian countryside. A few years back, Alma had a glimmer of hope his body was found, but after

DNA testing was performed on the bone marrow remains, it was established the body was her husband's brother.

Alma didn't understand. Her husband and his brother were taken away together with other village men. She asked questions from the forensics authorities but they had no conclusive answer. She heard from other women that the group of men was divided in two during transport. But no one knew anything for sure. Everything was wishful thinking. If her husband wasn't killed and buried together with his brother then where was he? It's been eight years. Was he on the other side of the world asking himself the same question about her, lost, with no purpose, searching for his brood? The throbbing in her temples, always in the background like a faint ticking of the wall clock, was a reminder that her mourning would never end.

In the fourth week of the notice to vacate, Alma found a place to rent. An older Bosnian woman called Minka, who was her co-worker at the cafe, said to Alma, 'I heard you might be on the street soon.'

Alma didn't like Minka, and she didn't know why. They'd both suffered during the war, yet an uneasy truce reigned between them. They rarely talked and when they did it was terse and work related.

Minka grabbed the handle of the wash tank, and with her tree trunk arms lifted the lid. Droplets of steam showered them. She pulled the tray with plates and slid it across the roller tracks to Alma. She put another load in, took off her gloves, and wiped her hands on a kitchen towel tucked behind her back. Somewhere from the depth of her enormous bosoms, Minka pulled a piece of paper on which she had pencilled a phone number and a name.

She told Alma a man called Ernesto was looking for someone to rent the bungalow at the back of his large property in St Albans. Ernesto lived alone.

Minka folded the piece of paper and put it in Alma's pocket.

Then, with both her hands, she took Alma's hand. She gave it a warm, gentle squeeze. 'Do you know why we can't stand looking at each other?' she asked Alma.

Alma shook her head.

'Because we remind each other of what we lost.'

'I thought it was hatred,' Alma said and Minka shook her head.

'I love how there is so much sunshine and warmth in this country, all year round,' Minka said. 'Very different from where we grew up. I love the Sun. I go to my backyard and let the Sun bathe me and kiss me. But after a while I feel my skin burning. Too much of what you love can be painful.'

In the evening, Alma called the number and arranged a meeting. Early the next day, she drove with her children to inspect the place. The morning was hot, and she opened all the windows in her old Corolla.

'How come we're the only ones driving with the windows down?' her daughter asked while she gawked at other cars.

'Because it is sooooo much fun to have wind in our hair,' Alma answered and shook her head. Her daughter did the same.

Alma parked in front of the house and waved at the man mowing the lawn in the front yard. Ernesto waved back and turned off the mower.

Ernesto was a man who had one of those faces that looked like there were too many teeth in his mouth. When he spoke he always looked like he smiled, an awkward, crooked grin like one of those that people involuntarily make out of despair.

They shook hands and introduced themselves.

Azra hid behind Alma, wrapping herself in her mother's skirt. When she heard how her mother introduced her, she jumped in front of Ernesto, extended her hand and said, 'I'm Ariel, like the mermaid. It's the name I wanted before I was born.' She gave her mother a look, pursing her lips and crossing her arms over her chest.

'You do have hair the same colour as Ariel,' Ernesto said. 'There's no mistaking she's yours. One doesn't often see hair as red as blood.' Ernesto marvelled at the sight.

Ernesto led them past the house where he lived. He told Alma he had had a wife and two grown up children but he lived alone now. They walked into the huge backyard. The grass was freshly cut and sparrows and starlings descended upon the lawn. Their little heads bobbed up and down as their bills pecked the grass, feeding on thousands of little insects the mower blades disturbed.

When the birds noticed them approaching, they lifted in the air as one, clicking their throats in unison. Alma watched the small flock disappear in the distance. Someone, she didn't remember who, told her the flock is the purpose, no matter how small. The bird is just a cell.

'They'll be back as soon as we're inside. They never give up,' Ernesto said and lifted his gaze. 'They're good for the garden. They eat all the insects and pests. But if you're growing vegies you better make sure you cover them with a net. They love seeds. Do you grow vegies?'

'No, not since I came to Australia.'

'Well, if we come to an agreement you can use all this.' Ernesto made a swipe with his hand showing his backyard. 'Plant anything you like.'

Alma still looked at the sky. The flock was circling above, waiting for them to leave.

'They say small birds like sparrows and starlings can live ten to fifteen years in the wild. Amazing, right?'

'That must be a lot in human years,' Alma said.

'I reckon.' Ernesto agreed. 'Sometimes I wonder if they look down at us and pity the way we live.'

Ernesto told her his father lived in the bungalow until he died in his sleep a fortnight ago, at the age of ninety-four.

'He was never seriously sick in his life. And then one night he stayed asleep.' Ernesto shrugged, his face puzzled.

The bungalow was a two-bedroom kit home made from fake timber and with a tin roof. At the back, there was a small porch and a backyard of sorts reaching to the fence. Inside, it was spotless. Ernesto told Alma his father was a clean freak.

Some of the old man's furniture was still inside. One bedroom was empty, just a couple of boxes Ernesto said he would take care of. In the other bedroom, there was a single bed and a wardrobe. Alma sat on it and bounced up and down.

'How much for the bed?' she asked.

'You can have all the furniture and a dog, if you like.'

'Dog?' Alma asked, confused.

'Let's sit and talk,' Ernesto said.

Alma followed him into the small kitchen, which also served as a dining area, and they sat at the table.

Ernesto said if Alma took care of his father's dog he'd offer a reduction in rent. Alma turned to see if her children heard, but it was too late. They were in the doorway, listening. They tugged at her shirt and pleaded with their eyes.

'Come, I'll show you the dog,' Ernesto said, and they followed him outside.

The dog was leashed next to his doghouse. He was a bona fide mongrel with five different colours on his coat.

Ernesto bemoaned, 'If you don't take him, I'm going to have to surrender him to the council.'

Alma didn't need another mouth to feed. The dog stood on his back legs, wagged his tail and lolled his tongue excitedly, as if he was aware of what was at stake. She asked for twenty dollars off the rent. Ernesto drew a breath and exhaled. He offered ten dollars less, and they agreed on fifteen and shook hands on it.

Ernesto smiled with relief and it was the biggest, widest smile Alma had ever seen.

'His name's Irving,' Ernesto said and handed Alma the keys. 'You can use my backyard anytime. He loves to play in there.'

He unleashed Irving, and the dog hurled himself at Alma. He stood on his back paws and put his front ones on her thigh. She knelt down and petted him. Her children gave him hugs and Edin threw a fake bone in the air for him to fetch.

That day Alma brought her belongings from the old flat, cleaned the bungalow and made it home. The children helped her unpack while Irving followed their every move.

When her children went to bed, Irving slept on his pillow in their room. When Alma came around to check on them, Irving was awake and she saw a mixture of sorrow and excitement in his brown eyes. A whimper escaped his throat.

Before she went to bed, Alma made herself a cup of chamomile tea and opened one of the boxes that was in the empty bedroom. It was full of photography books by one photographer, Irving Penn.

She opened a book randomly and viewed the portraits. Alma lay on her new bed, where the old man died just a few days ago, and looked at the images of people. Rich, pretty, glamorous, famous, poor, ugly, disfigured, big, small, happy, sad, old, young, white, black, brown. The photographer shot a great number of people. They were all familiar, yet she had never met any of them. She kept flicking the pages. Searching, looking, examining until her eyeballs strained to the point of pain.

In the late hours of the night, she fell asleep with the book on her chest and was dead to the world until the next morning. She woke up with lingering fragments of a dream. Images of people dancing flickered behind her eyelids. She held hands with someone. Or maybe someone held her hands, pulling her to opposite sides. Her children were on either side of the bed. Her daughter urged her to wake up. She closed her eyes, wanting the dream to continue or at least come back for a moment. She saw her feet running on a dusty road. Was she running or was she being chased?

Her daughter picked up the book and flicked the pages. 'I can't find a photo of daddy in this book,' she said to Alma.

The words shook Alma, and images flooded her mind. She saw her mother trying to hold her hands and stop her. She tore from her mother's grip and ran toward the trucks full of men being driven out of the village. She ran until she left a bloody trail on the dusty road like she was a wounded beast being chased. Her husband's face melted in the crowd of heads on the truck.

'He's not in there,' Edin said matter-of-factly. 'He's in a different book. We can have a look at it after breakfast.' He took his sister to the kitchen.

When Alma stood, she realised there were tears running down her cheeks. In the bathroom, she looked at herself in the mirror and for the first time in years, she saw herself for who she really was. A wounded beast still running.

—·—

It was Sunday and Alma set up her kids on a blanket and gave them watermelon to eat. She opened the gate between the two properties so that Irving could run around. She had to work in the cafe from four in the afternoon until ten at night. She was cooking when she heard her daughter cry.

After a short interrogation, she got to the truth. Azra ate her watermelon with a spoon and she spat the seeds toward Irving, who lay next to them. Edin asked her to stop, but she wouldn't. He wrestled the spoon out of her chubby little hands and threw it as far as he could. Irving stood up and pricked his ears. Azra ordered him to fetch, and the dog flew across the backyard. When Irving returned with the spoon between his jaws, Edin scolded him, and this made Azra cry like the rain. After Edin admitted what he did, he apologised and said he felt bad about it.

Alma calmed her daughter down and said to her son it was a good sign he felt bad. Edin looked at her.

'It means you care,' Alma said and extended her arm and her son embraced his mother and sister.

They stayed like that for some time until a scratchy voice jerked them back to reality.

An old man with a straw hat stood in their driveway. 'Your dog's been hit.' He pointed to the street with the pruning shears in his hand.

—ele—

Alma drove to the vet with the dog in her lap. Azra was crying in the backseat, while Edin craned his neck forward to get a look at Irving.

Alma patted Irving's neck and looked into his brown eyes. He was gripped by pain, but he didn't look scared. She was surprised he was still conscious.

The Vet moved his glasses on top of his head, stuck the x-ray on the light box on the wall and pointed at the spot where Irving's hind leg was broken between the fibula and tarsus.

Alma's children tugged at her skirt. Azra asked her what a fibula and tarsus were. The Vet brought a chair to the light box and put Azra to stand on it.

'This is the fibula and this down here is the tarsus.' He tapped something that seemed like a joint. 'This line here is the crack. That's the good news. I thought it was a break. No need to pin the bone. I just have to fix a cast for four weeks and expect a full recovery.'

Azra asked the vet why bones were called such funny names and he said that medicine was full of them.

'They're Latin words,' Edin said.

'That's correct, young man. The language of science.'

'Latin is a language?' Azra asked the vet.

'Yes. It's a dead language. No one uses it anymore, except in science, as I said.'

'Some churches still use it.' Edin said.

'Right you are again, young man,' the Vet said and smiled. 'You have a very smart boy here,' he said to Alma as he tapped Edin on the shoulder.

The Vet put Irving's hind leg into a cast, all the way up to his hip. He gave him two injections, and he fixed a see-through plastic cone around his neck. The Vet gave Irving a dog biscuit and said it could have been worse.

Alma told the receptionist she didn't have enough money to pay. All she had was fifty dollars, her last fifty dollars. An older woman flicking through the filing cabinet behind reception lifted her gaze.

'No problems. We will post you an invoice and you'll have a fortnight to pay,' the receptionist explained.

On the way back home, Edin and Azra talked about the fibula and tarsus. She said they sounded like names from her fairy books.

'Fairies don't exist,' Edin said.

'Yes,' Azra said, 'but if there were fairies, fibula would be the fat one and tarsus would be the naughty.'

Irving twisted his neck on his doggy pillow and tried to bite his cast, but the plastic cone did its job. Alma observed the dog she owned for just two days. An invoice to pay $560 arrived two days after they took him to the vet. She never had that much money in her bank account.

Alma dropped off Edin at school and went with her daughter to the vet clinic. She would talk to the vet clinic manager, a woman like her, probably with children. She would understand. Alma had seen her at reception the other day. She wore glasses, had a friendly face and gentle eyes. This woman, Alma hoped, would understand her situation. Alma would ask her for a payment plan. She could manage thirty, maybe forty dollars a week. Alma was sure the woman would accept this proposal. She had to.

It was hard leaving her children at five in the morning and going to the vet clinic to clean the kennels. It was only for two hours and only for a month, but she would have a rock in her throat during those two hours. Luckily, her son Edin was a smart boy. He'd wake up before his sister, prepare breakfast and get himself ready for school.

One morning after she finished her shift and was leaving, Alma saw Jonah waiting outside. Next to him was a small pet cage with a white, fluffy cat inside.

He greeted her, and she said hello.

'Just a regular checkup,' he pointed at the cage. 'Is your pet all right?'

Alma was dressed in the long navy blue overcoat she used for cleaning. Her cleaning gloves hung out of the side pockets. Her hair was in a bun and the pungent waft of sweat and kennel surrounded her.

'He is now.'

'A dog?' Jonah probed.

'Yes.'

'Where is he?'

'He's home,' Alma said and walked past him. She saw from his face he was trying to figure out what was going on.

'Did you manage to find a place?' he asked, and she knew this was what he really wanted to ask.

'We're not sleeping on the street,' Alma said and started for her car but stopped and turned. 'Not many students keep a pet?'

'It's my landlady's cat. Just doing a favour.'

Alma nodded. This time, she believed him.

She took off her cleaning uniform and sat in the car. She drank from a water bottle and called home. Her son answered and told her everything was all right.

There was a knock on the car window. Alma lifted her head, and Jonah was motioning for her to wind her window down.

'I quit my job at the real estate agency and got a job as a night filler in Safeway.' He took a deep breath and continued his speech as if he was worried he might forget what he wanted to say.

'My mate at Uni and I started this photographic business as a side gig to our studies. We specialize in portraiture. As a way of saying sorry I'd like to take a family portrait of you and your children. Free of charge. Whenever you want, if you're interested. Here's my card.'

'You're studying photography?'

'Final year, almost finished.'

Instinctively, Alma calculated his age. He was about three years younger than her. She took the card from him.

'I'll see,' she said and turned on the car. The car coughed and shook for a time and eventually, to Alma's relief, the engine flipped into life.

'Sure,' he said and waved as she drove off. She saw him in the rear-view mirror watching her. His hands were tucked in his pockets and he kicked something on the ground.

On her last day at the clinic, one of the vet nurses gave her cast-cutting scissors before she left. The nurse told Alma how to cut off the cast. The scissors looked no different from regular scissors, except the blades were on an angle and were all metal and solid.

'If you see anything unusual or he can't run or walk properly, bring him back,' the nurse said and Alma thanked her.

At home, Alma tripled up a piece of cardboard and made a few practice cuts with new scissors. Edin and Azra sat on the porch and watched the procedure, their feet kicking nervously in the air. Irving sat on the grass and thumped his tail in expectation. Alma went on her knees and let him sniff the scissors.

She told him what was about to happen. Irving licked her hand and barked. He was ready.

She ordered him to lie down and then she rolled him on the side.

'Hold him by the collar,' she told Edin, who was holding Irving's upper body.

'Be careful Mum.'

Alma gently slid the scissors under the cast, and Irving lifted his head, trying to get a look. He still had the cone around his neck. He whined. She put her hand on his belly and petted him. Irving trembled, but remained still.

With a hand made steady and strong from boning countless chicken thighs, Alma disposed of the cast in seven determined cuts. She told Edin to unsnap the plastic cone.

Irving stood up and gave his leg a thorough sniff. He then launched into biting the length of it, giving a four-week-old itch a thorough hiding.

'Let's see you run.' Alma threw his favourite toy bone as far as she could.

Irving stood still for the briefest of moments, not quite believing he could run. He chased after the bone and the children chased after him, screaming.

There was unbridled happiness oozing out of Irving as he rejoiced in his newfound freedom. She watched her children full of joy as they played with their dog.

Alma felt like the odd one out. She wasn't part of their little group. She was relieved the dog was all right, and that was it.

She lifted the cast with both her hands and it was heavy. Yes, she thought, this would make anyone grumpy. She could feel her spine stiffen and the skin on her back tighten, thinking of having something like that on her leg.

No, she wouldn't like having this on her leg, but she would endure. She felt that. She felt she could last four, six, eight weeks. However long it took.

She watched Irving drink water straight from the hose her children were playing with. They were all wet. Irving sucked on the hose like a person and drank water like he hadn't drunk in ages.

She would do that after the cast, Alma thought. She would run and jump and drink water straight from the hose. Alma could see herself, her face, hair and her blouse wet. She could feel the water filling her stomach and then spreading to every corner, rejuvenating her body. Something stirred inside her while she watched her family play.

Alma stood up, took off her sandals, pulled her hair tie out and ran toward her children and the dog. The flock was the purpose; she thought as grass prickled her soles.

She ran in circles with her children as Irving chased them. The ground was muddy and slippery and for an instant, she thought she was going to fall. But that would be okay. Alma wouldn't mind falling on the soft muddy grass and landing on her bottom. Her children would have a great laugh at that sight.

She sped up her run.

MAN STOPPER

One of my dad's mates, a fellow called Rebus, was getting locked up. He'd been in jail before, but this time he was going in for a good stretch.

Rebus was well known in the western suburbs. He grew up in Sunshine but the last few years he lived in a new house in Tarneit. My dad and Rebus were mates since they were little. Both their parents were from a land once called Yugoslavia. They told me how when they were kids they used to fight skips because of soccer. Neither of them ever got into Aussie Rules or cricket, although my dad spent all summer long in an old Footscray Bulldogs jumper. The jumper was from the days of Dougie Hawkins, probably worth a bit of money today.

When my mum asked him why he wore that old rag he said proudly, 'So that everyone knows where I come from.'

She replied, 'Footscray is not in the Balkans,' and my dad slapped her on the bum.

Later in their lives Rebus and my dad took separate paths. My dad chose the factory, got married and bought a house in St Albans. Rebus did anything but honest work, but they always stayed close.

Rebus was in his thirties when he got married. He and his wife never really clicked and over time he started bashing her. One day he went too far, and she ended up in Emergency. When his brother-in-law came to talk some sense into him, Rebus beat him up as well.

Rebus' brother-in-law knew how to throw a punch, a big fellow who'd been in plenty of fights, but Rebus sicked his mountain of a dog onto him, who pinned the guy to the ground. After that it was lights out for the poor bastard. They say Rebus broke both his knees with a piece of pipe. He'd never walk again properly. And the dog, he tore off one of his ears, but this guy didn't have the guts to report Rebus.

Rebus took his kid, his dog, set the house on fire and took off. Two days later the coppers cornered him on his property outside Sunbury, but not before he pulled a gun on them. After he was arrested the coppers went through his garage and the shed and found some shotguns, weed and a whole heap of stolen car parts. Now, Rebus will be lucky to get out before he's fifty.

Rebus' lawyer, a bastard as slick as a shaved swimmer and connected too, somehow managed to get him out on bail and on his last day of freedom he came to our house to say goodbye. He brought his dog, Bullet. Rebus and my dad sat on the back porch and talked over a beer and a smoke while I played with the dog.

Rebus told my dad he was angry he was going to jail because of pussy.

'If I'd only robbed a bank or gone out and got myself a whore. But my bitch wife wouldn't let me fuck her.'

'Yeah,' my dad said, 'shit we do to get some, hey.'

'Mate, she wasn't even much of a root,' Rebus said.

'Don't wanna upset you mate, we go a long way, but your wifey's got a great pair of tits.'

Rebus waved his hand. 'She does, but she's a dud in bed. Even when we were younger she was fucken crap. She screamed while we had sex, but not in a good way. Not like ooohmygodohmygodohmygod. Instead she screamed, 'Oh my God!' Rebus' voice went a few notches up the pitch scale. 'Like her baby's been trapped under a car.'

Rebus and my dad laughed. My mum came out with two more beers in one hand and the phone on her ear. She asked them what was so funny.

'Nothin',' my dad said, 'we're just talking about tits.'

'Pricks,' my mum said, shoved both cans into my dad's hands and went back to her conversation on the phone.

When they were done talking, Rebus called me over and asked me for a favour. He wanted me to look after Bullet while he was inside. Rebus said that I was the only human, apart from himself, Bullet liked and he knew I'd take care of him. I liked Bullet too, so I said yes.

Bullet was a huge dog. He was a Rottweiler and German Shepherd mix and the first thing Rebus told me about the dog was that he was trained to bring men down. No matter what their size or intent.

Rebus grabbed Bullet's face and stretched it. 'He's the reason no one fucks with me. They call beasts like him man stoppers. My beautiful monster.' He kissed the dog's muzzle. 'Look right into his eyes and you'll see what I mean.'

So I did. I stared at the dog and he stared back. I don't know for how long but it was a while. Bullet's face was anything but menacing. I could see both Rottie and Shep in him. I can't say I saw exactly what Rebus was talking about but I did notice one thing. Under that droopy face and relaxed body, a flame of constant alertness flickered. And you could only see it when he detected a noise or a movement that didn't quite fit into the frame of the three of us on the porch, like a cat coughing up a fur ball in the backyard next door or a baby crying a few houses away.

'You're safer with Bullet than with a dozen heavy-weight boxers.' Rebus took Bullet's head and pried open the dog's jaws. 'You see these.' Rebus ran his forefinger along the length of Bullet's front canines. 'When these lock onto something, there's no fucken letting go until you tell him to let go. Not even if Jesus himself came down from heaven.'

I touched Bullet's teeth. He seemed a little bored with all the attention and slobbered on my face. I put my fingertip right at the pointy end. Those weren't teeth. They were spears.

'And if you command him he'd rip Jesus to shreds too. Fucken weapon he is. Jimmy Finlan is history now. You can find that little carrot-top poofter and let Bullet make a garden salad out of his face. Or eat his dick.'

Jimmy Finlan lived two blocks away, north of Main Road West. A few months back, I stole Jimmy's bike. I knew it was his, and I still did it. Jimmy was in Brimbank Shopping Centre. He'd just leaned his new bike on the wall beside the entrance and went inside. Only Jimmy fucken Finlan would leave his brand new Mongoose BMX Fireball 26-inch unchained.

Jimmy and I had a history. It started when he was ten and I was six and he still lived in Hook Street, two houses away from mine. My football went over his back fence. I got it back slashed. This tit for tat went on for years until I stole Jimmy's bike. A couple of days afterwards he cornered me when I was leaving the milk bar. He had a knife and he took me to the laneway. Then he beat me up bad. I fell down on my stomach. He pressed my face to the ground.

'You little wog shit,' he said, 'it's time to fucken grow up. I'm the man now and it's time you learn that.' He pulled my pants down.

Every time he pushed himself inside me, Jimmy punched me. In the face, in my back, my ribs. I passed out from the blows. I came to around midnight. There was blood everywhere. On my face, hands, shirt. I tried to stand up, but the pain coming from my arse cut me in half. I dropped my pants and looked. It was like I had a period. I fished my phone out of my pants and called Rebus, but he never answered. Later, I found out he was shooting it out with the police.

As if he knew what I was thinking, Bullet butted his head against me. 'He doesn't look like a beast,' I said. 'I reckon he's just after some cuddles.' I couldn't resist teasing Rebus a little while his words about Bullet's strength and Jimmy swirled in my head.

'Cuddles, my arse. Looks are deceptive,' Rebus said.

I frowned and shook my head. I pretended I didn't know what deceptive meant.

'What are they teaching you in school these days, for fuck's sake.' Rebus shook his head. 'When he was a pup, I let him charge a man from fifty meters. It was a bet, and this cunt had a gun and managed to fire twice before Bullet was on his throat. I won the bet and gave him the name he's got now.'

I couldn't imagine the great mass of muscle and a head bigger than mine running, let alone being fast. I remembered reading that grizzlies are super fast over short distances, so who knows. Maybe Rebus wasn't talking shit. It didn't matter to me; I was glad to get Bullet.

Before he left, Rebus told me what to feed him. Then he said, 'The coppers, they think they can solve me. Fucken clueless cunts. Don't they know who I am? The great fucken Rebus.'

He laughed at this, but this time I really didn't understand what he was getting at.

'Christ on a crutch, kid. Tell me when it's your birthday and I'll send you a dictionary from inside. You need to open a book now and then.'

'Rebus means puzzle,' Dad said when I looked at him.

When Rebus and I shook hands, I asked him, 'How come you didn't let Bullet attack the coppers?'

'My son was sleeping with him in the back seat. Didn't have the heart to wake them.'

'Fair dinkum,' I said. 'They slept through all the commotion?'

'I slipped them both some Benadryl.'

'You're not supposed to—'

'I know,' Rebus interrupted. 'I wasn't supposed to do many things, mate.' He took a deep breath and pulled a piece of paper from his back pocket. 'Bullet responds to all regular dog commands in English,' Rebus said. He grasped my hand, 'except attack and release. I use German words for these and they are *fass* and *frei*. Here they are.' He then slapped the paper into my open palm.

'Got it. *Fass* and *frei*. Attack and release. No problems.' I looked at his writing and he took me by my shoulders.

'Now, this is important. It's not *fess*, and it's not *frey*. That's not how you say it. You've got to get it right. *Fass* is like when we say don't fuss and *frei* is like to fry eggs.'

Rebus let go of me and handed me the leash. He went down on his knees and hugged Bullet. 'Take care, mate,' Rebus whispered into his ears and the dog licked his face.

As Rebus walked away Bullet stood up and tried to follow but I said, stay and then sit, and he listened. After that I could only hear the tiniest squeaking whimper out of his throat like when you gently let the air out of a balloon.

That same afternoon, Bullet and I went for a walk. I was looking for Jimmy Finlan. I went all the way down Washington Street and then took a footpath through the man-made wetlands that separated St Albans and Cairnlea. I crossed the little wooden bridge over Kororoit Creek and turned left on the bike path along the fence where an explosives factory once stood. There was nothing there now. One brown circular building that was falling apart and a long row of magnificent blue gums standing as tall as giants. Bullet walked next to me as if he'd been down this road many times. A plane flew above us so low I could see the tyres. For a moment, I thought it was a huge bird of prey and I froze, but the plane quickly vanished in the distance.

I found Jimmy with a couple of guys from his crew sitting on the benches near the children's playground. His guys were playing cards and Jimmy was chatting up one of the girls that went to my high school. She was sitting on a swing and they were exchanging puffs of the same cigarette.

When he saw me Jimmy said, 'You little cunt, you forgot I fucken banned you from this park.'

'I came to change your mind about that,' I said and pointed at Bullet.

'What? You're gonna give me that fat mutt?'

'Just wanna show you what he can do first.'

Jimmy let the girl go and started walking toward me. I went down on my knees and put my mouth on Bullet's ear. Bullet was already on full alert. I patted his back and could feel his muscles tense.

One of Jimmy's guys jumped up and ran to Jimmy's side. He leaned into his ear and said something, and then he, his mate and the girl left in a hurry, leaving Jimmy alone.

'Is that Rebus' dog?' Jimmy asked. His voice wasn't cocky anymore. He put his right hand behind his back.

'Yep,' I said, 'and he hasn't eaten all day.'

I had trouble holding onto Bullet. He growled and kept rearing up onto his hind legs. Saliva dribbled out of the corners of his mouth. Jimmy took off his jacket, wrapped it around his left forearm, and pulled a knife from behind him.

'*Fass.*' I commanded, and Bullet took off.

Jimmy steadied himself and put his left elbow in front. He was going to let Bullet bite him and then try to stab him. Bullet reached Jimmy and stopped. He didn't jump or try to bite him. Instead, he started barking. Deafening, booming barks came out of his lungs. He danced around Jimmy, snapping his jaws in the air. Jimmy swung wildly with his knife and slowly started backing off, retreating toward the benches. It looked to me like Bullet knew exactly what he was doing. Maybe Rebus wasn't talking crap. Maybe the dog was trained.

Jimmy hit the table with his back and turned his head for a second to see what it was behind him. This was enough for Bullet. In the next moment, he was hanging off Jimmy's right arm. Jimmy dropped the knife and let out a scream. Bullet then yanked Jimmy's arm until he brought him to the ground. The dog jumped on his chest and put his jaws around Jimmy's throat.

Bullet waited for my next command. I stood above Jimmy. He was shivering. I kicked him in the nuts and he contorted in agony. Bullet held him to the ground. I stomped on his stomach and chest—once, twice, until there was no air left in his lungs.

I took the knife and pulled down Jimmy's pants. I looked around. It was dusk and there was no one in sight. At the nearest tree, I saw some ravens observing the show.

I cut out a piece of Jimmy's pants and wrapped it around my hand. I didn't want to touch his dirty dick. Jimmy lifted his groggy head, but Bullet closed his jaws on him again and this time a trickle of blood escaped.

I worked fast. I lifted his shrivelled balls and pulled them upward. The scrotum skin stretched. I slashed hard and cut off his balls like you would cut a weed off the ground. Blood shot up like water from a hot spring. He curled up and let out a long scream, followed by some deep grunting.

'*Frei*,' I said, and Bullet let go of Jimmy.

Jimmy's balls were still in my hand. I swung my arm and threw them under the tree where the ravens sat.

I started walking and Bullet stepped in beside me. When we were out on the street, I turned around. The screaming and grunting had stopped, and the shrill calls of ravens had begun.

I saw one raven land near the spot where Jimmy's balls were and start hitting the grass with its beak. The second raven touched down near Jimmy. It spread its wings and flapped them hard a few times, but Jimmy wasn't moving. A shriek tore through the air.

Then the rest of the ravens started landing.

TOMORROW

It's early March, a sunny Friday. My divorce papers are in the mail, but this doesn't stop my soon-to-be-ex-wife asking me to go with her to her friend's birthday party in Preston. We've been living apart for almost three months, but she still calls me a few times a week. There's always something: leaky taps or the garage door jammed. Just last week I was stapling posters with Roscoe's photo onto electricity poles.

Roscoe is our cat. My wife had him for five years before she met me. She brought him with her into the marriage and I've been cleaning up his piss, shit and fur-ball vomit ever since. In summer Roscoe would sleep at the foot of our bed next to my feet and in winter he'd wrap himself around my head. He's fifteen and has spent all his life inside the house and then last week he decided to chase a stray cat he sniffed in the backyard. Maybe he was thinking it was his last chance for a breath of freedom.

There are things I want to do around my new flat, I say to my wife. This is a lie. I'd set myself up with a television, fridge and new furniture within a week of moving out. Even gave the place a fresh coat of paint.

I can't face Jill by myself, she says.

Jill is her friend celebrating turning thirty-six. Jill has two daughters. My wife and I have no children. The fault is with me.

Shrapnel, a burning piece of metal from an anti-personnel mine, struck me in the groin during the war in Bosnia and they patched me up in a field hospital. The parts of my balls that produced sperm were burnt forever. Singed like two marshmallows in the hands of a drunken man over a campfire. My private bits were working, but because of the injury my sperm count was weak. If I had sex every day for the next thousand years the little suckers would never swim to where they were supposed to.

After ten years of trying to conceive, my wife said she had always wanted to have children. It was about being fulfilled; she said. She was still young and she loved children. Her pursuit would continue without me. After hearing this, relief spread through my veins as if I had just received a blood transfusion. I said I wouldn't stand in her way.

Anything about Roscoe? I try to steer the topic away from the party.

No, I would've told you, my wife says, but Jill invited me to this mother-daughter sleepover in two weeks' time. Can you fucking believe it? Four mothers and four daughters coming over to her house and she invites me. She reckons it would be good for me. You have to come with me. I'm not sure I'll keep it together at this stupid party.

We talk some more. She cries, she begs, and finally I give in to her.

There's a Bosnian bakery in Preston, on High Street, close to where Jill lives. I'm going to buy myself some *burek* and *baklava* to go with my all-night cricket watching.

I'm only staying for two hours, I tell my wife, and we're going by taxi.

Don't worry the party is in the early afternoon, she says, plenty of time to get home and watch the cricket.

It gets annoying being predictable. The first test match between South Africa and Australia played in Pretoria is starting tonight and I'm going to watch every ball bowled. And then, the plan is to sleep in until midday tomorrow.

We get to Jill's and the party is a wank fest. Some pricks I've never met are sloshed by three o'clock. Grog is served before finger food and it quickly fills empty bellies, making tongues loose. I don't drink, and I ate before I came. I know how it is at these parties.

A dickhead across the table wearing an *X-Files* t-shirt asks me why I'm not drinking. A faded mug of Agent Mulder is stretched across this guy's man-boobs.

Religious thing, right? he asks. Where are you from?

St Albans, I say.

No, I mean which country? You're not from around here.

I ignore this wanker.

Soon these people switch from footy and television to politics, religion and crap like that. They say things about asylum seekers and refugees. They touch on the war in Iraq and in Bosnia. They call the war a conflict. They don't know I was once a refugee. Between mouthfuls of sausage and beer they say heaps of rubbish.

I get up to leave but Agent Mulder yells after me and calls me rude.

I open my mouth, and the moment I do, I know it's a mistake. But it's too late. The dam inside me breaks and my words drown everyone on the table. It gets real ugly, but I feel real good.

Just before my yelling and fist-thumping reaches a crescendo, Jill's husband and my wife drag me out of the house.

Outside, while we wait for a taxi, my wife tells me that I embarrassed her. She's red in the face and her palms are sweaty. She wipes them on her thighs until she leaves wet marks on her dress, but I don't really listen. I was right. My wife knows it, Jill knows it, everyone at that table knows it, but God forbid you raise your voice and hit the table so you can be heard. Not in the company of those wankers.

There are ways to make your point without being rude, my wife says.

She doesn't think those people were rude. They were opinionated, but not rude. She thinks I was rude in making a scene.

This is your problem. Not your sperm count, she says. If you had any friends you would understand.

My friends aren't tosspots, I say.

They can't be tosspots or fuckwits or anything because they don't exist, she snaps back. Why do you always argue with drunkards? She asks me this like we're still married. But documents have been signed. The divorce letter will arrive any day. She's not my wife.

I cross the street and leave her.

You're the reason we're getting divorced, she yells after me. Not your dead sperm.

I walk to High Street and start looking for the Bosnian bakery, but I can't find it. Everything looks different. I try to remember the last time I was here. Five years ago? I get hungry. I find a kebab shop and order a chicken kebab with the lot with garlic sauce. I go outside and sit on one of the garden chairs in front of the shop and dig in. Sauce drips down my chin and I wipe it off with my sleeve. A guy in nice clothes sits next to me. He's quiet for a minute and then he asks me if I could spare five dollars. Not one or two, but five. I stand up and walk back into the shop.

While I eat, I look through the window. I used to know these parts. I lived in North Fitzroy, Northcote and then Thornbury. When my ex-wife and I were ready to buy a house, we couldn't afford it here. Cunts and tossers with deep pockets replaced wogs and students from the inner north. As I eat, I wonder if Nermin still lives around here.

I first met Nermin on the plane to Australia. The two of us and another thirty-four Bosnian refugees came to Melbourne in May 1994. It was the third year of the war. Nermin was ten years older than me. He told me on the plane he needed someone like me. Someone young and smart who could speak English. He said he was a maths professor back in Bosnia and he had big plans for Down Under.

Then, he said, you better smoke your cigarettes, because when we enter Australian airspace there won't be any smoking on the plane.

I told him, I don't smoke. He stuck a cigarette in my lips and said, What kind of Bosnian are you? I let him light the cigarette, but after I started coughing, he smoked it.

Nermin and I ended up renting a two-bedroom flat on Ford Street in East Brunswick. But before that we stayed for a month in government housing in Noble Park. There we saw the woes of the world. Refugees and asylum seekers from every corner of the world. We had to run away. It was too much like home.

Within a month of moving in together, Nermin bought a car. He said he always had a car and he couldn't imagine himself without one. It was an old, burgundy, two-door coupe, automatic shift Honda Prelude. He said he brought some money with him from Europe. There are ways to make money without using your back, he said.

Soon all sorts of people from the former Yugoslavia were coming and going through our flat. He was trying to bring his sister to Australia, chasing papers, making phone calls to the Department of Immigration. He spent all of his money on that.

I got a cleaning job in the Regent Hotel on Collins Street and started saving for a car. I sent some money to my sister, Fadila, in Bosnia. In a letter, I begged her to come over. She said she couldn't leave her boyfriend. Her boyfriend was shot in the stomach during the war and she was taking care of him. This happened shortly after I was evacuated through the tunnel under the airport runway.

In the meantime, Nermin organised all the paperwork for his sister. His sister just needed to pay for her airfare. In the same breath he said he had no money left and that everything he did for her was about to vanish.

I've got no one else to turn to, mate, he said. I hate to ask you, but you're like a brother to me.

We'd known each other less than a year at that point.

I'm good for it. Please help. He put his hand on my shoulder.

I told him he could sell his car. I needed my money so I could bring my own sister. He knew this.

Brother, I got jibbed, he said. That car's a dud. No cunt would buy it. Trust me on this. I bloody tried.

He put me on the spot. My sister still hadn't made up her mind, but that could have changed at any time. This I knew.

I gave him all of the three grand I'd saved up. A couple of days later, I came back from work and found Nermin had moved out. I heard later he was living in Preston with his sister. I never got my money back.

When my sister's boyfriend passed away, Fadila said she couldn't come because a stray dog had a litter in the garage and she had to take care of them. Then it was the house, which was in disrepair, she said. The roof needed fixing. Then she asked me, if she came to live with me, who would take care of our parents' graves? Years went by in a correspondence like this.

Then one day, not that long ago, she said she was too old to go anywhere now.

I cross High Street and head for the side streets. I remember one of the streets leads to the Bell train station and if I follow that street I'll get to Nermin's house. Walking slowly, I check out the houses and front yards. Then I see a burgandy Honda Prelude. I open the gate and walk up the steps of the small porch. There is no answer when I knock on the door. I call out. Nothing. I walk around the house, up the driveway to the back-yard. I peek over the fence and see a man with long, grey hair wearing only his shorts, digging a hole. Something is wrapped up in a blanket next to the hole. I recognise a large U-shaped scar on the right side of the man's abdomen. It's Ermin. He'd told me it was a knife wound he suffered in hand-to-hand combat. Later he revealed the scar was from a rudimentary removal of an inflamed gallbladder full of gallstones, done somewhere in the woods of eastern Bosnia while he was running away from *chetniks*.

Because of this operation, Nermin had trouble with his stomach and always ate lots of vegetables and fruit. One day, while we still lived together, he brought home two mangoes. I had never eaten a mango, and I grabbed a small kitchen knife and started peeling the skin.

Slow down, peasant. That's not how you eat mango, he said. He took the knife from me and cut the sides and then sliced the exposed flesh into cubes, which he ate off the skin.

All I can think, as I watch Nermin dig the hole, is that I shouldn't be here. He's really into digging. He swaps between pick and shovel. He's got a method. The hole's getting bigger by the minute. Whatever is wrapped up in that blanket could almost fit in the hole. I decide to leave, but I can't move. My shoes are glued to the ground.

What are you doing here? I hear Ermin.

It's me, mate.

I know who it is. His angry voice bounces in my eardrums and spreads to my temples.

I see an old, gaunt man with a face hidden behind a bushy beard. It's Ermin, but it's not him.

I'm busy, mate. Nermin points at the hole with his shovel. What do you want?

Had something to do on this side. Thought I might stop and see how you are going.

Nermin drops his shovel and puts on his singlet. He walks over to me.

Listen, he starts, about the —

Not why I'm here. I cut him short. What's with the hole?

My dog died early this morning.

Sorry.

He was old. Been sick for a while, something with his lungs.

Nermin doesn't look like a drunken, angry man who once provoked a hall full of equally plastered Bosnians. Most of them were refugees like us, and one of the drunks scoffed at how a maths professor was one of them now and soon would be forced to work in a factory. In return, Nermin wished *chetniks* raped their females before killing them all. They were in shock by Nermin's words just long enough for me to take him out and drive off.

How are you doing? I ask.

My dog died, that's how I'm doing.

Your sister? She still lives with you?

She drowned in the Yarra a few years back.

Sorry. I didn't know, I say.

It wasn't on purpose. A truck hit her from behind and she flew off the bridge. Nermin opens the gate to his backyard and lets me in.

I'd offer you a shovel, but I only have one.

How about I dig for a while and you take a rest?

Thanks. I'm almost done.

Can I see your dog?

Haven't you seen enough dead?

People only, but no dogs, I answer.

I still remember seeing my parents dead, putting their body parts in bed linen and then taking them in a wheelbarrow to be buried. They were waiting in a bread line when the shell struck.

But I don't remember seeing any dead dogs. Or cats. I'm sure many of them died from bombing and machine gun fire. Most animals disappeared when the war started. Those that were trapped with us during the siege of Sarajevo looked like skeletal ghosts of the past. And when they were ready to die from hunger, they would just find a hole and die. Alone.

People, dogs, same thing, Nermin says.

What happened, mate? I can't resist asking.

Nermin takes the shovel by the top of the shaft and sticks the blade into the ground. There are droplets of blood coming out of his cracked palms. Mud is stuck under his fingernails. I look at his face hidden behind the beard and notice red scaly psoriasis patches in the corner of his lips, under his ears and eyes.

Darkness ate me, Nermin says and puts his dog in the hole.

Nermin shovels back the earth, and I walk back to the station. It starts to rain and I hide under a tree. A girl in her early twenties does the same. We nod at each other and our lips stretch in that awkward half smile. After that we don't look at each other. She's pretty. Blonde hair. Blue eyes. Milky skin. Like the first girl I ever met here in Australia. Like my ex-wife.

When the rain stops and before she walks away, I ask the girl if she knows where the bakery is. She tells me to follow her. She takes me through a little park and behind the town hall.

They make great pita, she says as she points at the shop.

When I get home, I find a letter with my divorce papers in the letterbox. It's finished. I'm no longer married. Time to watch cricket.

I take off my shoes in the hallway and see the flashing light on the answering machine. I press the button and hear the voice of my officially ex-wife.

Roscoe is dead, she cries. He was found on the street, a block away from our house. A car hit him. I need you to come and help me dig a hole in the backyard, she says. There's a short pause and I can hear my ex-wife sobbing.

I'll try calling again a little later. Then she takes a deep breath. No, scratch that, you watch cricket tonight. Tomorrow. I'll try again tomorrow.

I pick up the phone and start dialling her number.

CROCODILE

It was ten at night, and Saltie was late. I paced in circles while my mate Sheppard watched muted television. Me walking didn't bother him. Every time I heard a car on the street, I went to the window and peeked through the curtains.

'What's the movie about?' I asked Sheppard.

'The end of the world.'

On the screen, a group of astronauts were getting ready to intercept an asteroid hurtling toward Earth. They were hugging their crying wives and sweethearts.

'Where's Rondo?' I asked. Rondo was Sheppard's grinning dog.

'With your mum.'

I went to my mum's bedroom. Rondo was next to her on the bed. She had her hand on his back. My mum had chronic bone inflammation. It had started after I was born. Over time, her bones thickened and got swollen and then later became distorted. Her arms and legs were bowed and arched, her fingers crooked. She couldn't walk properly anymore. A nurse, who came twice a week, showed me how to wash my mother in case I had to. How do you wash a human pretzel?

She spent a lot of time in bed or if the weather was nice at the back porch looking at our bare backyard. Her view was one dead apricot tree and a rotting cubby house. She knew about the animals in the shed. There were six large dog cages and six smaller ones, for cats or rabbits, full most of the time. I also had a few birdcages. She would open her mouth, lift her crooked finger and point, but no words ever came out.

I touched her forehead. Her special water bottle, with a long bendy straw, was on the floor. It landed right next to her bedpan, which was empty. I cleaned the straw and left the bottle next to her face.

Rondo came with me to the living room and sat next to Sheppard who gave him a slice of pizza.

Saltie had called late in the afternoon and said he would come to my place around six. He ran things in the western suburbs. From Footscray to Melton, no one so much as farted without him knowing. Saltie is the guy you had to wait for.

He was vague on the phone. I told him my shed was pretty quiet at the moment and that tomorrow I had only one delivery to make in case he needed my van.

'It's not about Janice,' Saltie cut through my rambling.

Janice was Saltie's niece. She looked like a model but had problems in her head. She left me a couple of weeks ago.

Saltie said he needed my skills for an upcoming job and to make sure Sheppard was with me. 'Gonna have to put your noggins together.'

I was uneasy around Saltie. Like his niece, Saltie had mental problems. Maybe it ran in the family.

I called Sheppard and told him about the phone call.

'Relax,' Sheppard said, 'he just needs a dog.'

I asked him to bring beer and pizza.

Sheppard's my partner. They call us dog nappers. We're a small outfit, two men and Sheppard's stumpy mutt, Rondo. I didn't like being called a dog napper—we never demanded a ransom for the dogs we stole. We sold them. And we didn't steal just dogs, but also cats, rabbits, turtles, snakes, hamsters and birds. People were usually after pedigree cats and dogs. I never asked why they needed the other animals.

Like any job, it was mundane at times. Once we had to travel up the Hume Highway to Euroa and steal a pygmy pig. The guy who hired us told us it was his wife's pet. They got divorced. She ended up with a large property in the country.

'At least I'll have some bacon out of this divorce,' the guy said while counting our fee.

The pig didn't want to leave my arms. Poor bugger knew his time was up.

This guy must have threatened he'd do something to the piggy because Sheppard told me he found it locked up in a large, wire-mesh enclosure. He had to use bolt cutters to get in.

Since Sheppard came on board, I hadn't been doing the stealing. Too risky. I did everything else: I handled prospective customers, made deliveries, and fed the animals in the kennel; I waited in the van and I drive; and I told Sheppard if trouble came while he was on a job I'd leave him behind. He laughed. I told him I was serious and he laughed again. He gently slapped my cheek. I'd known Sheppard for six years, and I still couldn't read him.

I first met him in the Youth Justice Centre. After we'd got out, we did a couple of years of high school, before dropping out. Sheppard was a translation of his surname in Bosnian. We lost touch and then I saw him again when I delivered dogs for this dog-fighting joint outside Rockbank. This guy who ran the joint needed half a dozen dogs. Any dogs.

'For the warm up,' he said. He paid good money. So I grabbed the first six mongrels I found on the street or in front yards.

That was where I saw Sheppard. He had a dog with him he was going to put up to fight. He had no job and was still living with his sister in Deer Park. I offered he come work with me and he said yes. Instead, that night, Sheppard and his dog, Rondo, jumped into my van and they've been with me ever since.

I joked once about how I saved Rondo's life that night. Sheppard casually replied that Rondo had had six fights, won them all, and killed four dogs. My eyes widened. Rondo was a cross between a sausage dog, a red heeler and who knows what else. Short, bulky, and brown. When Sheppard saw doubt in my eyes, he said, 'Rondo's a weapon.'

We serviced a cross-section of society but only via recommendation. Which meant someone we trusted had to vouch for the customer. I didn't want to be locked up again. When you're behind the fence, things happen no matter how hard you try to keep safe. These things, they stay with you. They're like cobwebs in the corners of a doorway. You clean them, but in the morning they're back in the same place.

Sheppard and I took a fifty percent deposit before every job and collected the rest upon delivery. In the western suburbs, we stole pit bulls and American staffies for dickwads who thought these dogs made them look tough, or for dumbos who thought they would protect them in case of trouble. The first lot were often as shady as we were and the second lot usually had a wagonload of children.

Everyone knew children and pit bulls didn't mix, but that wasn't my problem. Sheppard didn't share this view. He reckoned all dogs were good. It was people that made them bad. Maybe he was right. I didn't care. I did what I had to do, for me.

Across the Yarra, we sold the odd pit bull, but it was mostly exotic breeds people were after over there. Like Japanese Spitz or Clumber Spaniel. Once we travelled to Sydney to nick a walking mop of a dog called a komondor. The hairy mutt was sleeping on the back porch right in front of the backdoor and we nearly stepped on him thinking he was a shoe rug. We were in a posh suburb, so I quickly stabbed the dog with a syringe full of Telazol. He fell fast asleep.

I got the drug from a vet on Station Road in exchange for prescription food for cats and dogs. We stole the food from a warehouse in Altona. Animals ate this food when they had some health issue. Like, they couldn't cough up fur balls or had recurring urinary tract infections. You could buy this food only at the vet's. I got enough sedative to last me a few years.

Lots of jobs came through Janice. She knew a whole heap of dropkicks. Tradies, builders and their women rolling in money from the housing boom in the west.

The day before she left me, Janice brought this scrawny woman and her four-year-old daughter to my place. She said the woman was a housemaid, cleaning flats and houses around Carlton and Fitzroy.

The woman had $100 and the dog she needed was kept in the Children's Hospital Research Centre. She explained her daughter had a deadly nut allergy. If she ate anything containing peanuts or almonds, she went into anaphylactic shock and could die within minutes. The hospital had four companion dogs trained to sniff out the smallest traces of nuts in food. They were selling them for ten grand.

'These dogs,' the woman said, 'lift their paw as a warning when they smell nuts.'

While she talked, the little girl put her lips to her mother's ear and asked her who I was.

'He's the boy who's going to bring you your birthday present,' her mother said.

'I want the golden doggie,' the girl said.

One of the dogs was a goldendoodle, a golden retriever and poodle cross. The mother showed me a photo of her daughter with the dog. They had the same colour hair.

Sheppard got in touch with one his mates who worked as a security guard in the hospital. We waited a few days until he was on night shift and now goldendoodle was in my shed waiting to be reunited with allergy girl. I planned to do that tomorrow.

The mother and her sick daughter were the exception. By and large, people were scum buckets like us and were cheapskates to boot.

Another service we provided was removal of the microchip. I would locate the chip under the skin, usually on the back of the neck, make the incision with a Stanley knife and squeeze it out with my finger. I had to use pincer pliers a couple of times. A little while back, I got a bullmastiff drunk with a cheap cask wine and Sheppard and I still had to wrestle him to pull the metal fucker out.

I walked outside into the backyard, leaving Sheppard watching mute television. I figured Saltie needed my shed. He probably wanted to use it to stash something or someone or, and I hoped this wasn't the case, he wanted it for one of his torture sessions.

Saltie was a psychopath and a standover man with connections to dodgy bosses in the dockers' union. There were stories going around that he could speed up or slow down the unloading of containers for a fee.

Saltie got his nickname after he apparently wrestled to death a saltwater crocodile somewhere up in Cape York Peninsula. I saw him play soccer once. He was wearing only shorts. There was a large, dark green croc tattoo on his chest. The spiky tail looped around one nipple and its open jaws enclosed the other.

Saltie had no neck and had a shock of unruly black hair. His upper body was disproportionately muscular to his matchstick legs. He reminded me of an illustration I saw in an old book about demons that was on my bookshelf. I remembered the image because it looked ridiculous. It was the last demon listed in the book. The creature was depicted as having a large owl body and long, thin legs. His name was Stolas, the Great Prince of Hell. And Saltie was the Great Crook of the West.

Saltie always carried a pair of crocodile clips and some wires. Just like in the movies, he connected the wires to power points and the clips to humans.

Once, Saltie tied his crocodile clips to a rope and clipped them onto the testicles of some poor bastard who owed him money. He tied a barbell to the other end of the rope, which he placed into this fellow's mouth. Then he made him stand on the table until gravity did its job.

This thing with Saltie paying me a visit was a long time coming. I started having a bad feeling about my animal operation a few months back. With every animal we stole and sold, I felt this invisible pressure closing in on me like a giant, rusty vice grip. It was inching ever so close to my chest where it was going to crush my rib cage like dried up twigs. At times, I struggled to get enough air in my lungs.

I took a deep breath. It was a starless night. Weakness ran through my joints as if I had a fever. I sat on the steps of the back porch. There was movement on the back fence. A black and white cat that belonged to my neighbour jumped off the fence and dragged itself along the concrete path that ran through the middle of the yard. It came to me and rubbed its face on my shins. I picked it up and patted it. The name on the tag read Mitzi. She purred heavily as she kneaded my knees and parked her fat body in my lap. I touched her belly and felt movement inside. I made a mental note to talk to my shithead neighbour tomorrow.

I came back inside and sat on the sofa next to Sheppard. The movie was finished and there were men chasing an egg-shaped ball. Sheppard and Rondo were chewing on a pizza crust.

I looked around my living room. It wasn't the place I wanted to be in. For a long time, I was on the fringes, doing my own thing. Content. Invisible. Now, I was waiting for a criminal psychopath to arrive at my house. Sheppard was sipping his beer and Rondo had his eyes closed, a toothy grin still on his muzzle.

Two things had led to this moment.

I was a one-man operation and then, a couple of years back, too much work started coming my way. Wannabe yuppies from the outer west that were living in their mansions built in three months, who usually craved pit bulls or American Staffies, started ordering pedigree breeds they couldn't even pronounce. No man could steal that many dogs alone so I got Sheppard to work with me. This put me on Saltie's radar.

The second thing was that Janice left me. She left me for a guy who bred pit bulls on a property outside Melton. Pit bulls were in constant demand in the west. Instead of stealing them, I paid a guy to breed them for me. I made an arrangement with this Greek fellow and I asked Janice to pick up a pit bull pup for me. The next day, she moved out. Then that night Saltie called and said I was late paying protection money. While I was with Janice, I didn't have to pay.

I asked him if he could give me another week and that I'd pay extra interest. I told him I was behind with my mother's medical bills. This was true. He hung up on me while I talked and I hadn't heard from him until today.

Maybe Saltie thought it was my fault Janice left me. I should have listened to Sheppard. He told me not to date her.

Sheppard said, 'I'm not telling you because she's Saltie's niece, but because she's a whore. She's a mega fucking whore. And you know how I know she's a whore? Cause, a couple of months ago, she came into Burton's with cum on her chin and ordered a gin and tonic. How do you not know that there is cum on your face? She's touched up here.' Sheppard slapped his forehead.

I'd heard stories about Janice, but she was like the reddest rose you've ever seen in the middle of a weed-infested garden. And she fucked like a banshee. She'd do things other girls wouldn't. She was nasty, and I liked nasty. No hole was sacred. She'd make me fuck her in the bushes next to the oval behind my old high school during recess. Boys came and watched us humping and she'd urge them to pull their dicks out and wank. I'd protested, started getting limp. She said if I stopped she'd let the boys gangbang her. I was relieved when she dumped me. Of course, it didn't look good in Saltie's eyes. Who knows what she told him?

Saltie arrived four hours late, walking into my place with two of his thugs. He was in a blue singlet, trackie dacks and thongs. He liked to show off his upper body. There was no flab on his chest or arms.

He greeted us and asked us if we'd had dinner.

'Pizza,' Sheppard pointed at the coffee table.

Saltie took the remote control from Sheppard's hand and switched the channel to the cricket. He sat between Sheppard and me and for half an hour and watched highlights of the day's play. England was touring. It was the Ashes.

I didn't know he followed cricket. People who liked cricket were patient and methodical, I'd heard. This must be true for sadists, too. Sweat beaded on my forehead. Invisible pins danced on my stiff neck.

Saltie swore when he heard Ponting got out cheaply. I glanced up and down his body. There were scars everywhere. Saltie had been slashed down his face, had a claw hammer put through his brain, shiv in the kidneys, icepick in his right knee, got peppered by a shotgun in the back. He was tall, lean, and taut. If you didn't know about his stick legs, he looked like a mini white version of LeBron James. Deadly, like a bullet.

'A couple of years ago, I booked myself and my missus into one of those cricket touring parties with the old folks,' Saltie started. 'You travel around England and watch cricket in between. But my missus said no. She was due to pop out our daughter and wouldn't let me go. She said if I missed the birth of another child, I'd better stay in England. I was in prison when my son was born. Having a father is important. What do you reckon?' Saltie tapped my knee.

Saltie'd seen my father in Barwon Prison two years ago. He said my father was in cahoots with some Irishmen and was doing all right for an old fellow. The mob always meant more to my father than his own family.

'He'd like it if you visited.' Fake concern stained Saltie's words.

'That's what I keep telling him,' Sheppard butted in. 'Your old man isn't getting any younger.'

'You should listen to your mate Shep here,' Saltie said. 'He knows what loss is. Or maybe you don't care when people in your life leave.'

Fucking Janice, I knew it.

'Do you know how your father died?' Saltie asked Sheppard.

Sheppard shook his head. His father was killed in a concentration camp run by Serbs. Sheppard told me how one day he took some bread and water to the camp and the guard took the bread and started eating it. The guard then told him that there was no need for him to come anymore. He never saw his father again.

'I hope it was quick,' Saltie, a man intimate with inflicting pain, said.

'Me too,' Sheppard said.

'You have a sister, Samira, right? She works for my lawyer.'

'Yes. Studying law.'

Sheppard, his older sister, and his mother came to Melbourne as refugees. They settled in St Albans. Soon after, their mother died. Her heart stopped in her sleep. They got sent to two separate foster homes. When his sister turned eighteen, she got Sheppard, and they rented a flat off Main Road West.

'She's too nice for this part of town.' Saltie winked at me.

Sheppard shrugged his shoulders, trying to look cool, but he pulled Rondo by the collar and brought him to his knees. He rubbed the dog's neck. Rondo pulled his tongue in, his grin disappeared and he locked his gaze onto Saltie.

'Some fellows around here think that I'm losing my edge. That I'm becoming nice, like your sister. Except I don't have her curves,' Saltie winked again while running his palms along the sides of his torso and hips.

Saltie told us some fellows stopped paying and one of them was going around making fun of certain parts of his physique.

'It's my fault. One time I gave a guy extra time to pay and now every cunt thinks I'm running a bloody charity.' Saltie squeezed my shoulder when he said this.

This, Saltie said, was damaging his reputation. He reckoned there were some people out there—he waved his tattooed hand right above my head when he said this and it looked like he made the sign of the cross in the air—who thought he was getting soft. He had an obligation to uphold his standing. For his next job, he needed a special 'tool'.

'I've decided to live up to my nickname. This is where you two dog nappers come into play.'

I glanced at Sheppard. He was calm again. There wasn't a trace of worry on his face. He looked eager, impatient to hear what this tool was. He grinned just like his dog Rondo when he was excited. I looked to see if there was a wagging tail attached to Sheppard's bum. The thing was, and this was what really bothered me, I didn't know if Sheppard was faking his eagerness, in which case he'd get points for being smart, or if he was really that fucking dumb. I couldn't tell. I liked to think it was the former, but there was this happy and at the same time vacant expression on his mug that made me tense.

Saltie got up and walked behind the sofa. He put one hand on my head and the other on Sheppard's.

'I want a baby crocodile by tomorrow night. Six pm sharp.' He clunked our heads together.

Rondo growled, but Sheppard shut his muzzle with his hand.

Saltie snapped his fingers and one of his men went outside. He came back with a fruit basket.

'For your mother,' Saltie said, and he left.

That was it. We had to find a baby crocodile for Saltie in less than twenty-four hours.

Baby crocs weren't pets. Not in Melbourne, anyway. Sheppard and I, we'd done a few snakes and a turtle in the past.

Recently, a capuchin monkey who never stopped grinning, just like Rondo, who always had a half-snarl/half-grin expression on his chunky face. You didn't know if he liked you or wanted to rip you to bits.

Sheppard learned from me how to steal a pedigree cat or dog off the street or from a backyard. He was good at breaking into pet shops at night or stealing dogs from a vet shop. I wasn't worried about the stealing part. If there was a baby croc out there that needed to be stolen, we could find it. It was the time frame. Finding a Labrador in a day would be a problem. Saltie always gave people tight deadlines. He was generous with us.

Sheppard stayed the night at my place. In the morning, we drank instant coffee and ate plain toast. We were in a spot. For a time we didn't talk, then Sheppard said he had to go home and drop off his niece to kindergarten.

'I didn't know Samira had a child,' I said.

'Yeah, a daughter. She's four,' Sheppard said. 'Do you think Saltie knows?' It was the first time I saw a shadow of fear on his face.

'Probably,' I said. 'I'll come with you.'

Before we left, I peeked into my mother's bedroom. Her chest slowly moved up and down.

⁓ℓℓℓ⁓

Samira's daughter was a little blonde and blue-eyed angel. She'd gotten her mother's looks. Sheppard unbuckled his niece from the child seat and carried her out. They walked into the building holding hands. A few minutes later Sheppard came out carrying a piece of paper.

'I had to sign a permission slip for this.' He gave me a one-page brochure for a mobile reptile farm visiting the childcare that afternoon. There was a photo of a bearded codger with a fat snake wrapped around his neck, holding some type of lizard in one hand and a baby croc in the other. The farm was a one-man operation.

'There'll be a baby croc there, they said.'

Sheppard and I agreed we couldn't bring the croc to my shed. I didn't want to unsettle the animals I had in the shed. We had two dogs and two cats in there. Not a big number for us, but one of the dogs was a bloody Husky. As big as a tractor and not coping with the heat very well. Heat made him cranky and I couldn't keep him in the cage all day long.

The guy who paid a deposit for the dog had cancelled the order. Apparently, he'd read that Huskies didn't mix well with small children. He had a one-year-old baby. Instead, he put in an order for a pit bull. What a dick! I was having trouble off-loading the Husky. He'd been with me for nearly a month and was starting to think I was his new owner. The other dog was the goldendoodle, the gentlest dog I've ever seen.

I had to make sure Sheppard didn't steal an iguana or gecko or something else. Hours slipped by and the last thing I needed was to be late for Saltie.

We decided Sheppard would nick the croc, and I'd deliver the goldendoodle to Broadmeadows. We'd meet at the oval behind the high school. Whoever came first would wait.

The image of the allergy girl cuddling her new dog still floated in my head when I heard Sheppard whistling. I needed to squint to see Rondo and him trudging across the burnt grass as puffs of dust swelled up around their feet. The sun was behind their backs and they looked like sharp shadows that had escaped a nightmare. Rondo's studded collar reflected the last traces of sun and it looked like fairies were dancing around his grinning head. Rondo was like his master, unpredictable and distant. Perhaps that was the reason Sheppard kept him.

'No more of this crocodile hunter bullshit. I don't care what Saltie or anyone else wants,' Sheppard said when he came close.

There were fresh scratches on his forearms. He chucked the bag in front of my feet. The bag thrashed and Rondo barked and jumped on the bag as he tried to bite it. Sheppard stuck his foot into his ribs, scolded him, and the mongrel quietened. I'd never seen him be rough with Rondo. He must have had trouble with the croc or the bearded old-timer.

'Did you tape his jaws?'

Sheppard nodded and lifted his arms in the air. I unzipped the bag a little and peered inside.

'Careful, he's small but springy.'

The croc's head lunged toward my face, startling me. I dropped the bag on the ground. The baby crocodile wriggled itself out of his canvas prison. Immediately, he assumed a fighting stance. Rondo stiffened and stopped grinning.

Sheppard prodded the croc with his foot, and a throated hiss came out of his open jaws.

I carefully grabbed the croc by the neck and body and looked into his eyes.

I knew a little about crocodiles. The big ones with all their armour looked built to last. When I looked at the little croc I knew he wasn't supposed to be here. I didn't mean with Sheppard and me on the oval, but in general. His kind should have been wiped out with the rest of the dinosaurs. But I wasn't sure if crocs were part of that family. They looked like they didn't belong to our time. They were nature's contradiction.

I held something alive and scaly that was the length of my arm and that would grow to five or six metres in the wild. The croc was as still as a stake. I remembered watching a doco about crocs being patient creatures. How they basked near water with their jaws open for hours. How a mother crocodile was gentle with her offspring, carrying a bunch of babies in her mouth to the water. The mother would open her jaws and gently move her head from side to side so that the water washed the sand from her babies' bodies.

I knew they had two pairs of eyelids. I stared, but the little croc didn't blink. His eyes were green, and the pupils were thin black strips. It felt like I was holding a statue.

Then I saw the masking tape.

'You put the wrong fucking tape on his jaws.' I lifted my hand to smack Sheppard, but he ducked in time.

The croc felt pressure on his body ease and he made his move. He wriggled out, and I felt his smooth belly and ragged back slip through my hand. The croc fell on the ground; the tape came off and I heard his jaws snap free.

'Couldn't find gaffer tape, mate. I taped it half a dozen times. I'm not picking him up again,' Sheppard said.

'Like fuck you're not. If we don't deliver him tonight, it'll be crocodile clips on our balls,' I said.

While we argued, the croc took off across the field. The little bugger was smart and fast.

Double-quick Rondo caught up with him and locked his jaws around his head. He wildly shook the small body. When it went limp, he ran back, dropped it in front of us and grinned.

The lifeless body fell, raising a cloud of dust that travelled upward, reaching my balls, and they shrank like someone stuck them in an ice bucket.

MAHALA

Today is the first Sunday of the month, and for my dad and me it's movie day. Ever since the war finished, we watch an old videotape once a month after breakfast. We found it in the rubble of the top storey of our house. We've seen it together thirty-six times. The last few times it almost didn't happen. Dad was busy on the day. He asked me to watch it alone. Maybe my dad is ready to move on, but I still need to see my mother.

My dad is in the bathroom panting and muttering. He goes quiet for a bit and then starts again, cursing over the racket of his tools. When I peer in I see he's lying in the bathtub. There's an old towel under his head and he's on his back like a car mechanic, trying to fix the hot water tank. The tank is mounted on the wall. The bottom nearly reaches the tub-edge where all the pipes, dials and handles are. We lost our hot water this morning and he's been at it all day.

I'm studying in my room. Tomorrow I've got an oral exam in biology. Last week, our teacher reached the letter O in the class roll. My surname starts with P. Tomorrow, I will stand in front of the class and draw a piece of paper with a question on it from the teacher's jar.

It used to be a lolly jar that belonged to her son. He died on the line. She told us he was twenty. They buried his body on the school's football pitch. I can see the pitch through the classroom's windows.

We're learning about human anatomy and the exam questions will be about that. Last week, one student drew a question about the intestines and our teacher began crying. While she sobbed, she told us her son was hit in the stomach. Small shrapnel, no bigger than a walnut, ripped through him.

My wish is not to get a question about the stomach. I also wish I could see my mother's grave from my window, and that my dad stops working on the tank so we can watch the tape.

We only watch the first two minutes. In the tape, a choir of young girls is getting ready to sing. You can see the back of a woman, her long, strawberry blonde hair curling halfway down her back. The woman clears her throat. She says, 'ready,' her voice clear and resolute like a school bell.

The girls straighten their backs and lift their heads slightly upwards. They look at the woman and wait for her signal. The woman counts three, two, one, but it's really quiet and you have to strain your ears to hear it. She lifts her graceful hands in the air and the room explodes in one voice that is high pitched and booming at the same time.

The girls are singing their school's hymn. It's an upbeat, fast song that talks about hard-working students that walk to school through sun, rain and snow with their heavy school bags on their young shoulders. But the bags aren't heavy, the song says, because they're full of knowledge and the children's brains are thirsty for it. The children are carrying their school bags full of schoolbooks and those books will carry them into the bright future where all possibilities can be overcome, even a war. But the song says nothing about what the war is.

It's a regular school hymn and now I know it's full of hogwash. I know the text by heart, but I don't listen to it anymore. Nor do I watch the girl's faces. I don't know what my dad sees, but I imagine it's the same as me. I watch those hands, the strawberry blond hair, and the bracelet dancing around the woman's wrist as her hands glide through the air. It's all I see. It's all I want to see today. They are my mother's hands.

My dad asks me to go to our neighbour Emir to get some tools. He's going to be longer than he thought. I suggest I make us some sandwiches and tea, but he declines. He says first he'll fix the hot water and then we'll watch the tape. I said nothing about the tape, but he knows what I'm thinking.

I don't mind going over to Emir's so I can see my friend Rizo too. Emir is Rizo's uncle and they live together. I write what my dad needs on a piece of paper. I don't want to bring the wrong thing and have to go again.

I go to leave but he tells me to wait. He peers through a small bathroom window.

'Still snowing' he says, and I nod.

'Go upstairs and see if Emir's car is in their driveway. If the car's not there, don't go.'

Dad rarely lets me go upstairs on my own. It's still a mess and, in my father's mind, a hazard. He thinks I might trip and fall off the house.

My dad and I live on the bottom floor of our house. Or what's left of our house. Our *mahala*, our neighbourhood, one of the many sprinkled across the slopes at the outskirts of the city, received the brunt of the siege. Most houses in our mahala were damaged during the war. Many were used as military posts or machine-gun nests by both sides.

At the end of May, in the first year of the war, a direct hit destroyed the top floor. The bomb pierced the roof and exploded inside. It killed my mother and wounded my father in his right leg. He limps and in winter when snow falls and makes the earth white, he can't feel anything below the knee. I was physically unharmed. We kept our family albums on the top floor, but no photos survived.

Now, three years after the war, nothing remains upstairs. In spring, a swallow pair comes and nestles in the roof remnants until early autumn. Then they leave and in winter the only thing that lives there is snow.

We have everything we need on the bottom floor. There is a kitchen, bathroom with toilet, a living room where my dad sleeps and another room where I sleep.

I walk up the steps and push the lid to the side that my dad made to cover the opening of the top floor. Some snow falls inside. Our house is on a hill above Sarajevo and in summer we have a magnificent view of the city in the valley. In winter, like today, smog covers the valley like a grey fluffy eiderdown. It's hard to imagine there is a city underneath.

I see Emir's yellow Škoda in front of their house. I come down the stairs. Half way down, I turn and pull the lid back. I put on my boots, jacket, beanie and gloves and I walk out into the whiteness. War scars that are still visible on the streets are covered partially, for a time, until spring.

There are four empty houses between Emir's house and us. They're just shells with no windows or roofs. One of them is burnt to the ground.

Halfway to Emir's house, I meet my schoolmate Selma. She's one year younger than me.

'I can't find Whitey,' Selma says, standing on the street, looking left and right.

Whitey is her pet rooster. His plumage is as white as snow, except for his tail, which has a few black feathers. Whitey is a handsome bird with flaming red wattles and a straight ten centimetre high comb.

'I found this in the backyard.' Selma opens her hand and I see a few black feathers. 'I'm afraid dog wanderers took him.'

Dog wanderers, former pets still mad from war, are a problem in the outer suburbs. They roam the streets, hungry and sick, all skin and bones looking for human scraps. Authorities have neither money nor the desire to do anything about them.

'Last night was pretty stormy. I didn't hear any dogs howling,' I say to Selma. They always howl at night when they're in our mahala. They announce their arrival, giving humans a chance to leave the streets. And we do. We retreat inside and if we have to go out it's usually in pairs and armed with sticks.

Selma turns her head to her right so she can hear me better. She's a refugee from Srebrenica and during the war she got an ear infection. There were no antibiotics for treatment and her eardrum burst, leaving her with permanent damage. Now, she always has a piece of cotton wool in her right ear.

'I'll let you know if I see him.' I don't know what else to say.

'Wait,' Selma says and reaches into her pocket. She pulls out a handful of seeds and she empties them into my jacket pocket.

Before I leave, I ask her how her family is. She lives with her mother, two sisters and a grandmother. There are no men left in her family. Her brother's body was found in a mass grave, but there's still no trace of her father's remains.

Selma's mother sometimes cooks for us. She brings us large pots of beef and vegetable stew or *sarmas* carefully rolled in cabbage leaves. Then my dad and Selma's mother talk about Selma and me. A few months ago when she visited, Selma's mother said she checked with the City Council and she was told the minimum legal age for marriage is eighteen years.

'Unless the girl is pregnant. In that case, it drops to sixteen,' she added.

My dad raised his eyebrows and straightened his back.

'Let the children be,' he said. 'There's plenty of time for grandchildren.'

After that Selma's mother stopped coming for a few months. She turned up again a week ago with meat *burek*, acting like nothing ever happened.

—ele—

I leave Selma and arrive at Rizo's house. Rizo, like Selma, is also a refugee. He arrived at the beginning of the war from Višegrad. His father was taken by *četniks* and hasn't been seen since. A sniper killed his mother while they were escaping. His uncle Emir, a student in Sarajevo, took him in. They became our neighbours when the University hostel burnt to the ground and they moved into the house next to us. We heard that our previous neighbours are somewhere in California. They left this place just in time.

Rizo told me when his mother got hit, they were running with a group of refugees across the paddock. He said he thought she tripped because she fell on her knees. Then her face fell into the grass and a pool of blood formed around her head. Rizo knelt beside her, but a man grabbed him and carried him into the woods. He restrained Rizo from running back onto the field.

All the refugees dispersed, but this man stayed with him. After midnight, they went to his mother's body and dragged her into the woods. Her hands were cold, her face bloodied. After they put her under a tree and covered her with branches and leaves, they recited prayers for the dead.

The man told Rizo that the area was called Mare's Head. 'If you survive the war, you can come and look for her and give her proper burial,' he said. He took a small knife out of his pocket and asked her name, and cut her initials into the tree.

Rizo and I went after the war and found the tree, but we didn't find her body. There was no grave, or clothing, or bones. Just grass. I looked up at the wild cherry tree's canopy. There was a bird sitting on a branch, but I couldn't recognise it. Maybe it was a woodpecker.

Afterwards we went to Rizo's village. There was a small supermarket with a car park. Rizo said his house was somewhere under the car park, but he wasn't sure. He was little when he left and a lot of time had passed. In the bus on the way back to Sarajevo, Rizo cried in his sleep. Not long after, Rizo went to the office of International Commission of Missing Persons and they took a blood sample from him. They would use it to match DNA in case they come across his father's body in one of the mass graves.

⁂

Rizo waits for me at the front door of his house. He says he saw me coming. He asks me about Selma and I tell him about Whitey. I give him half of the seeds.

'Come, I just made coffee.'

In their living room, Emir is filling little half cups with coffee.

'Your mate Rizo will never learn how to make good coffee. Look at this,' Emir lifts the *džezva*, a long-necked coffee pot with a long handle, 'Look how weak this coffee is. There's no sediment at the bottom. A fortune-teller couldn't tell anything from this.'

'Come on, uncle Emir.' Rizo waves him off. 'It's not good to be superstitious.'

'Why not?'

'It brings bad luck,' Rizo answers.

It takes a moment for his pun to hit and we all, as one, burst into laughter.

'You watched the tape today?' Emir asks while we drink coffee.

The whole neighbourhood knows about our ritual.

'Not yet.' I tell him about the hot water tank and the tools I need from him.

Emir gets up. 'Have a cup while I get the tools.'

On my way home, I stop in front of Selma's house. I look around, hoping to see her rooster. Instead, I see Selma in the window. Her face is pressed to the glass, and it gets foggy quickly. She uses her sleeve to wipe the glass. I walk into her front yard and lift my head and eyebrows. She shakes her head. Her eyes are red. I say I'm sorry and she waves at me.

———

That evening I go to bed early reciting paragraphs from my biology textbook. I have to go to school in an unwashed school uniform. There is no point washing it in cold water. Maybe my dad was right. Maybe, right now, hot water is more important than the tape.

I fall asleep early, listening to the clamour of tools and curses coming from the bathroom. Whitey comes into my dream. He is huge and Selma and I are riding him. At first Whitey just walks, but soon he runs. He flaps his wings, trying to fly, and as he takes off, I fall off him. I watch from the ground as Selma and Whitey fly off into the grey sky. Whitey makes a sharp loop and then swoops down toward me. Selma extends her arms and grabs me.

I feel a hand on my chest, and I wake up.

'It's nearly midnight. Let's watch the tape,' my dad says.

I rub sleep out of my eyes, get up and nod. 'Have you fixed the water?'

'Try the tap.' There is a satisfied grin on my dad's face.

I go to the kitchen and see Selma sitting at the table. Whitey is in her lap, eyes closed, and she's petting him.

'Where did you find him?' I ask her.

'Rizo found him. He was in Emir's Škoda.'

'That backseat must be real cosy on a day like this,' my dad says.

I turn on the hot water tap and put my hand under the stream. After a few seconds I feel warmth on my skin. I stop the water, not wanting to get burnt.

'I'd like to watch the tape with you,' Selma says.

We both look at my dad and he waves at us to come. A tired smile escapes the corners of his mouth.

'All right,' I say, 'but you know you can't see her face.'
'I know.' Selma says.

—ℓℓ—

Dad, Selma and I watch the tape. We're on the couch with Selma between us. Whitey is on her lap. His eyes are still closed. My dad is supporting his head with his hand. He looks like he'll fall asleep any second.

I don't know what they see.

For me, it's always the same. I don't watch the faces of the children in the choir. Their faces are a blur and the singing is just background noise for those beautiful, elegant hands. They move graciously through the air, guiding those little heavenly voices. They move and I can feel the air around my face moving gently. It caresses me, kisses me, and plays with my hair. Once again, I feel my mother's touch.

Two minutes pass quickly. They always do. The football game that someone taped over the choir performance starts. I've seen those two minutes so many times, but it is always a shock to be brought back. I feel Selma's hand on mine.

'She was beautiful,' Selma says and squeezes my hand. Her touch is warm, soothing.

I nod and let her warmth penetrate my skin.

NAMES OF WILDFLOWERS

Rick Webber thought he was my boss and called me by a name that wasn't mine. He said he couldn't be stuffed trying to learn how to say my name properly. I never got upset with Rick. Not even when he called me a white wog and a Bosnian bastard.

Rick was about three times my age and had worked the same job, riding a forklift and shifting pallets, for the past twenty-odd years. He was born here, in Melbourne's West. Maybe he reckoned that gave him rank. Or maybe he was just an old grump.

The two of us worked in a warehouse at the end of Leakes Road in Werribee. It was where the city stopped and the country started. Most buildings in the new industrial estate were still empty. It was a ghost town during the day. Who knows what it was at night?

In a few of the places there were unleashed dogs patrolling the yards. You could see them during the day. I saw a Rottweiler in one and a pair of Dobermans in another.

In the yard, the Dobermans guarded there was a Running Postman plant, its long shrub stretching from one side of the building almost to the fence. The little pairs of scarlet pea flowers dotted the thick, light green mat of leaves that covered the ground. I tried to reach the flowers through the fence using a stick, but had no luck. The Dobermans came closer and observed me. They made no sound. I hadn't breached their territory yet. They sat on their haunches, two statues of muscle and bone with docked tails and cropped ears. They sure looked like they would have made a running postman out of me if I tried anything more.

At the warehouse, Rick told me what to do and how to do it, and I listened for the most part. The job had to be done no matter what Rick, or I thought. Our pay was the same, no matter what Rick imagined. And our boss popped in unannounced every couple of days, so we had to have each other's backs. Apart from the boss, delivery truck drivers were the only people we saw and talked to. As for Rick and me, we only spoke when we had to. It was all job related. And then six months ago Rick's wife died.

~oOo~

When I first met Rick, I was twenty-one and in my first year of university. Ten years earlier, my mother and I had arrived as refugees to Melbourne straight out of the hell of Sarajevo's siege. The freezing, sleepless nights on the streets of Vienna were hidden deep inside my brain, resurfacing when I least expected. We stayed briefly in the Austrian capital, trying to go to America, England, Holland and even Argentina, but we kept getting knock-backs from embassies and consulates. Then we heard that Australia had lowered visa requirements for people displaced by the Bosnian war.

I took my mother's reluctant hand, and we trudged from Wien Südbahnhof train station to the embassy on Mattiellistrasse. Slush ice filled my leaky boots. While we waited in the embassy corridor packed with people like us, my mother took off my boots and put them under the radiator to dry.

As I filled out the forms, my mother was still unsure about the whole thing.

'It is too far,' she said as she looked at the map of the world on the wall. My mother touched Australia. 'Is anyone even sure this place is real?'

A few months later, when we touched down at Tullamarine Airport, she found out the land down under was real. We were lucky enough to receive permanent residency visas. I later discovered it was our relatively good health and my knowledge of English that pushed us over the line. The practical things that help you find your feet in a new country were the deciding factor. Not the level of suffering one had endured, as we had thought.

Our destination was the Gold Coast, but we were told no spots were left in refugee accommodation there for another three months. They asked if we wanted to go to Melbourne instead. We didn't really care or know the difference. We just wanted out of Europe, as far as possible, from the land where half our family were buried.

'Yes we do,' I said.

An embassy official took us into an office, where he issued us with our visas. We had no passports, so visas were attached to a light green, A4 size piece of paper that said *Document to travel to Australia*. On one side there was a large stamp with a kangaroo and an emu, on the other was our photograph. I held the green paper of freedom. It was as light as a couple of feathers.

While he was writing things down, the official said, 'We have programs that re-unite families affected by war. Do you expect any other members of your family to join you in the near future?'

'Only in the other world, God willing,' my mother said. I explained to the official that my father and sister were dead and we had no one else.

We left three days later with one bag each. In my bag I had my sister's herbarium, which the customs officers found upon landing. They told us it had to be quarantined. One custom official referred to it as the flower book.

A month later, I got the book back and for nearly ten years it sat on the shelf of our glass cupboard between the two remaining photographs of our whole family and my mother's collection of Turkish demitasse coffee cups. Underneath, and on every shelf, were intricate crocheted doilies, tablecloths and potholders my mother made after her shifts as a dishwasher in a restaurant on Station Road.

It was only when I was in my uni class and the lecturer said we should start a herbarium that I brought it out. Now that I study botany this flower book has come in very handy. I studied part time in the afternoons because we could not afford for me to study full time. When my shifts at Bunnings started clashing with my classes, I had to find something else. One of the Bosnian women my mother knew told her about an opening at a new warehouse close to where we lived. So I got a job there as a storeman, driving a forklift and receiving and despatching goods.

At the same time, they transferred Rick to set up the operation. When my boss introduced us, Rick said, 'There's no way I can say that wog name.' He looked me up and down and came close to my face.

I smelled tuna on his breath. Rick had of one those heads that looked like an egg with sideburns and dark, restless eyes.

'You look like a James to me. I'll call you Jim,' Rick said.

Later, I noticed that most words longer than two syllables presented a challenge for Rick. In time, he called me Jim, Jimbo, Jimmy, Jay, Jamesey, and Jimbaroo. None of these were remotely close to my real name.

The only time words came out of Rick's mouth clear and proper was when he was swearing. He could curse through a mouthful of pie and chips, but words would come across as clear as a newsreader.

And this included several smut words he insisted I teach him. Rick couldn't say my name, but he could tell you to fuck your own arse in perfect Bosnian. He even mastered the body language and facial expression to go with it. He was very proud of his 'angry wog' impersonation.

After the introductions, our boss left and Rick sat me down in the lunchroom. He said that because he just met me, he would call me a cunt. He said that everyone's a cunt unless they proved otherwise. In his book, he said, there were five stages of friendship or respect. The order was Cunt, Faggot, Wanker, Dickhead and Brother.

Most people stayed cunts forever, he said. So he called pretty much everyone a cunt except truckies. To their faces, he called them brothers. He said you don't fuck around with cunts like truckies.

'Those cunts are connected,' Rick said, 'plus they bring all sorts of goodies here. You never know your luck.'

When an Indian delivery driver brought us a pallet of A4 paper reams that had been soaked wet, he signed the delivery docket and said to him, 'Don't worry brother, we'll take care of this.'

He then took the driver to the side and spoke to him for a bit. When Rick came back, he said, 'That brown goat fucker better come through.'

Every Thursday for the next two months, the Indian truck driver brought Rick a different Indian meal for lunch. Rick had curries, kormas, naan bread and butter chicken, all with saffron rice as yellow as the Slender Buttercup wildflower.

After Rick tried the first meal, he said, 'The Paki's wife can cook.' He then ranted about the rubbish he'd heard on the six o'clock news. No inner censorship, just a river of crap.

I let him rant.

One Wednesday, I came to work and Rick's car wasn't there. He always came before me. Soon, I received a phone call from my boss who told me Rick's wife had passed away and that Rick wouldn't be in for the rest of the week.

I'd met Rick's wife on a few brief occasions. She came to work when he forgot to bring his glasses or hadn't taken his blood pressure pills. Her name was Mary, and she had a firm handshake for a woman her age.

The next Monday, Rick came back to work. That whole week, he mostly sat at his desk or went behind the building for long periods of time. He would return with his eyes red, a purple face and wet sleeves. Our boss found him like that once but said nothing. The boss asked him how he was doing and Rick responded with a customary 'not bad.' Then they spoke about the weather or the footy.

I watched Rick all this time and on a day when I finally saw him make himself a cup of tea; I did the same. I got the chocolate scotch finger biscuits out of my locker and sat close to him in the lunchroom.

Before he could get up and leave, I said, 'My sister was killed in the war. She was six. Her name was Amela.'

Our eyes briefly met before Rick stood and left. At the end of the day before he left, Rick said, 'I'm sorry.'

A few days after this, Rick joined me in the lunchroom.

'Your father was killed in the war, too.'

'Yes,' I said.

'The boss, he told me.'

I nodded. Rick rubbed his hands, not meeting my gaze.

'Rick,' I said, 'we're having dolmas for dinner. Do you want to come tonight to my place?'

'Who's we?'

'My mother and I. She's a great cook.'

'I'm sure she is, but I don't eat wog food.' He looked up at me. 'No offence.'

I could hardly believe my ears. Rick had almost apologised for something he said.

'What about the Indian food? You didn't seem to have a problem gobbling up all those curries.'

Rick cracked a smile. 'Not tonight.' He stood up to leave.

'Don't fight it,' I said. 'Let it take all of you until nothing's left inside.'

He stood at the door, not turning around. I could almost hear my words bouncing inside his head like ping-pongs on a table.

And then, when I thought he would leave, Rick turned around. 'What's with all those flowers lined up on the table at the back?' He waved toward the far end of the warehouse.

'They're for my assignment in school.'

'I thought you were at university.'

'I am.'

'Don't tell me you need a degree to be a florist these days.'

'I'm studying botany.'

'Botany! Christ on a fucken cracker.'

'It's the science of ...' I tried to offer an explanation.

'I know what the fuck botany is. Plants! Trees, grass and bloody flowers.'

'Yes.'

'Well, from today you're officially not a cunt anymore. You've just promoted yourself into the Faggot category, faggot.'

I smiled. 'Thanks Rick. It's a privilege.'

'Can't fucken believe it. How are you going to make a living from fucken flowers?'

'I'll find a way.'

'My hairy arse, you will. Flowers are for ladies.'

'Botany is not just about flowers.'

Rick shook his head.

'How much more do you have? You nearly done learning?'

'Not until I count all the seeds of a poppy plant,' I said and Rick laughed.

<hr>

Shortly after this Rick came to work all smoke and roar. I asked him what the problem was.

'Fucken neighbours. Sticking their noses into my shit.'

'What happened?'

'This bastard living next to me came to my door yesterday and asked me if I needed help with my garden. Fucken nerve of that guy. Should have kicked him in the guts.'

Rick clenched his fist and punched the air.

I wasn't sure what was going on, so I stayed silent. As always, Rick continued to rant.

'Before Mary died, all I ever did around the yard was mowing the lawn. My wife was into gardening and compost and water saving and all that crap. Neighbours would come and admire her garden and she would talk about how much water we saved. She would pull out the water bill and show them the back of it, where they tell you about your usage. You know that shit about how many litres per person, per day the household saved.'

'Okay,' I said.

'So I haven't done anything since the funeral. The place is a bloody jungle. This guy pissed me off so much yesterday, so I started mowing everything in sight. Hard fucken yakka, it was. The night came quickly. I couldn't see properly, so I turned on all the outside lights and got some floodlights from the garage that made my place look like it was Christmas. I was mowing and whipper snipping until about ten when the police came and told me to stop. Apparently, I was causing a disturbance. Gave me a verbal caution. Fucken hell.'

'I could come and help you finish.'

'Thanks, but it's almost done. I fucked up big time.'

'Don't worry about it. It was an impulse.'

'No, I mean, this is not what Mary would've wanted.'

'Your garden probably needs some rejuvenation. It's good to do that every few years.' I tried to comfort Rick.

'You reckon?' Rick's eyes lifted.

'Sure. When you're ready, I can fix you up with some seeds.'

'Yeah. Mary would like that, I think.'

'Mary was a good woman,' I said, even though I didn't really know her.

'Yes, she was,' Rick said. 'She still ended up dying in her piss, blood and vomit.'

'We all do.'

'I'm not sure if I'd like to go like Mary. They told me it was fairly quick, but I didn't buy it. I found her lying on the floor when I got back home. She must have been struggling all day. They said she had a blood clot somewhere which travelled to her lungs.' Rick tapped his chest.

'If I had to go, I wouldn't mind going like that,' I said.

'I think I'd prefer a bullet to the head instead of a blocked artery.'

'That's how my sister went.'

'She did?'

'It was a sniper.'

For a long time, Rick didn't say anything. We went back to the warehouse and worked. Rick sat at his desk and sorted out purchase orders, delivery dockets and invoices from a pile of papers on his desk. I jumped on the forklift and brought the pallets I unloaded off a truck earlier that day.

Before lunchtime, Rick came to me and asked if the gas bottle on the forklift needed changing.

'I changed it yesterday,' I said.

Rick went behind and checked if the bottle was sitting properly. Then he said, 'It's not the same, you know, dying at sixty and dying at six.'

'I know.'

'What kind of coward shoots a child with a sniper rifle?'

'People like us,' I said.

'What do you mean? I would never —' Rick protested.

'I mean, the guy who shot my sister was a regular, ordinary person like you and me. He was a shopkeeper before the war.'

'You knew him?'

'Yes, we knew him very well. His shop was on the way to our school. He and my father were schoolmates.'

I remembered a tall, cheerful man who always gave my sister and me lollies or Animal Kingdom chocolate bars when we stopped to buy something. Our father had long conversations with the tall man and we played behind the shop with his children. The tall man also had a boy and a girl. On the back wall of the shop, above the liquor and cigarettes, there were two high-powered air rifles, together with some framed plaques of rewards and men holding rifles. The tall man was vice president of the Gallery Rifle Shooting Club. Soon after the war started, there were rumours he was a sniper. We all knew he was on the other side. Then one day, our side captured a couple of their soldiers who confirmed the rumours. Our surprise was only temporary.

'Did you guys find him?'

'No. We heard he left the country just before the war ended.'

'Anyone can be anything,' Rick said.

I silently agreed with Rick. Anyone can be anything. Anyone can be a monster. And a monster can be anywhere.

'Did you see it happen? Was it in the house?'

'No, I just heard a shot. Didn't think any of it. There was machine gun fire and bombs falling that whole day.' I got off the forklift and walked to the roller door. Rick followed. I pressed the button, and the door started going up.

'My father was on the line fighting and my mother was a nurse. She was in a hospital doing her shift,' I continued.

'They left you alone?' Rick was amazed.

'No, we were in our cellar hiding together with another three families. I was ten at the time. My only job was to keep an eye on her.'

'What happened?'

No one ever asked me a direct question about this. Many wanted to know, but their concern was only a disguise for their thirst for the macabre. So I told Rick the whole thing.

I told him this:

The cellar was small, four by five meters. Twelve scared and hungry people were inside. We ate from the same pot and we slept in turns on each other's shoulders. The bombing could last for hours. One time we were in hiding for three straight days. When we walked outside, the sun burnt our eyes, and I felt a pain in my pupils for the rest of the day, like someone had poured boiling water in them. One woman had a small baby and all the adults took turns trying to calm it. Our body smells merged into one suffocating, stink cloud that filled the room.

When you had to pee or shit, you went behind a blanket in the corner. My sister had trouble going. During the lull in fighting, she snuck out. One moment she was curled up next to me, and then the next she wasn't. We found her outside on our front lawn with a handful of golden lilies from the garden. They covered our front lawn every late spring.

'Aren't lilies weed?' Rick looked at his boots.

'They're wildflowers. They're way too pretty to be called weed.'

'I'm not sure my wife would approve of them in her garden. She had a thing against anything she didn't sow. She spent hours in the garden around this time of the year. Preparing the ground, weeding, digging, mulching. And while she planted, she would pant and moan.'

'Moan?'

'Yeah, she would moan and groan and make all sorts of sounds. If you were just listening to her without seeing her, you would be forgiven for thinking she was doing something else,' Rick chuckled. He stopped talking as he remembered something in the past, and I let him drift away. After a time, he shook his head and we walked outside.

'My sister loved flowers,' I said. 'She kept this herbarium where she collected a whole heap of them. She made sure they were all dried and properly preserved before she mounted and covered them with plastic with all of their leaves beautifully spread.'

My sister took great care of her herbarium. My parents gave it to her on her fifth birthday after seeing how much she liked collecting flowers. It was leather-bound and handmade by a bookbinder from Baščaršija, Sarajevo's old bazaar.

In the bottom section of every page where you put data about the plant like its name, date, and place found, my sister would write the name of the flower and things like *there were bees collecting the nectar* or *I had to use scissors to get this one.*

'That book would be handy for your studies now,' Rick said.

'I still have it. It's half full and I'm slowly filling the rest of the pages.'

Rick nodded, and we both looked into the distance. I saw a bunch of blue gums sprinkled on the green rolling hills that extended as far as my eyes could see. For a moment, I expected to see a large dust cloud approaching. I imagined myself squinting and waiting for a herd of cattle or sheep to emerge out of the dust cloud chased by nipping heelers or circling kelpies.

Instead, a small hill, a kilometre or so away, vibrated in sunshine. Tiny specks of various colours, like a rainbow sprinkled on the grass, shimmered in the distance under the two gum trees that stood atop it.

It was the first nice day of spring, so Rick and I went outside to eat our lunch. We sat on plastic garden chairs and lifted our faces toward the sun as we chewed. I ate a turkey sandwich and Rick had his leftover pasta bake. We drank raspberry syrup mixed with mineral water.

Rick asked me to top up his glass. 'Jimmy, pour one for us will you'?' Rick referred to himself in plural when he needed something; in singular when he was taking credit for the work we did together. After I topped up his glass, Rick said, 'Nice day, innit?' He lifted his hand toward the sky.

I nodded. I preferred warmer weather and hated days when you had to run the heater all day long. Ours was one of those old gas heaters that took up half the living room. I had to break my back to get it started and once I got the pilot light going, I never touched it again during winter. The heater could warm up the two-bedroom unit we were renting before you could make your toast and tea, but I had reservations about it. I heard all these horror stories in the news about whole families being suffocated by carbon monoxide because of faulty gas heaters. When I told my mother about it, she just shrugged.

I didn't tell her about my plans yet. If everything kept going the way it was, we would be moving out before the year's end into something better and bigger. Maybe even into a house with a bit of a backyard where I could plant something. A nice day like today was perfect to start a garden. It was like one of those days we had in the middle of summer back in Sarajevo.

'You had days like this back in Bosnia?' Sometimes Rick flipped through my head like he was reading a newspaper.

'High summer only,' I said.

'You miss the snow?'

'No, not the snow.'

'Good, nostalgia is the mark of a primitive man,' Rick spat out the line from his book of wisdom.

'I miss other things.'

'You wanker, you just ruined the moment. You should have kept your gob shut.'

I had progressed on Rick's scale of friendship.

'Don't you think I deserve to be promoted to dickhead?' I asked.

Rick looked at me for a while. He rubbed his face and sighed deeply.

'I think you're right. I'll call you dickhead from today, but I'll doubt you'll ever get to be called a brother.'

'I hope you're wrong.'

'Me too,' Rick said.

'We should go for a walk one day,' I said.

'Where to?'

'You see that small hill? The one with two gum trees on it.'
Rick nodded.

'We should go there. It looks pretty from here. I've been looking at it for some time now,' I said.

'You want to see what kind of plants you can find there, right?' Rick read my mind again.

'I've got a pretty good idea what's out there, but yes.'

Rick didn't say anything. He stretched in his chair and put his hands behind his head. He was soaking in the sunshine. He didn't say anything for a long time.

I put my cap on my eyes and slowly drifted off. I had a few minutes of sleep and dreamt about my sister and me at the swimming pool. We were having swimming lessons. My sister learnt to swim before me. I watched her do a perfect freestyle, taking in the air every four strokes, her face looking at the ceiling when she did it. In the meantime, the instructor was holding me by my shoulders while I was doing my chicken, aeroplane, soldier moves trying to master the backstroke.

I woke up with Rick's hands on my shoulders. He shook me. I saw binoculars hanging around his neck.

'That hill you're talking about, there are all sorts of colours there under those two trees. It was like our garden when Mary was still here.'

'If I didn't know any better, I'd say you just had a moment of a primitive man,' I told Rick.

'Guilty as charged,' Rick admitted. 'Fuck it, let's go now. We did most of the work for today. Get a bottle of water for us, will you?'

⸺⸺

By the time Rick and I reached the bottom of the hill, we were pouring sweat.

We walked up the little hill. When we got to the top we stood and looked at the rolling hills and solitary gums interspersed here and there. In the opposite direction in the distance, we saw the tiny buildings of the city. Washed in the sunshine, they didn't look real.

We turned around slowly until we completed a full circle. It was a really pretty spot. Rick sat down under the tree.

'I told you,' Rick said, 'flowers everywhere.'

'Yep,' I said and cast my eyes on the carpet of grass with dozens and dozens of different types of wildflowers.

'It's almost like they shouldn't be together. All these flowers in one spot,' Rick said. 'I'm sure some of them can't live next to each other.'

I took a closer look and noticed examples of competing species. I saw billy-buttons, wrinklewort, sun-orchids, milk-maids, early-nancies, buttercups, blue pincushions and many others. I quickly counted more than thirty species. They were all grassland species of the Victorian Volcanic plain that started in Melbourne and stretched all the way past Port Fairy in the west. Rick was right. They were common to see, but not all in one spot. It was almost like someone planted them all on this hill. But that didn't make sense. Even if it were true, not all these wildflowers would thrive next to each other.

I told Rick that the spot was a bit unusual.

'They shouldn't all be here. I knew it!' Rick said.

'No, they shouldn't.'

'You reckon your sister and my wife would like this place?' Rick asked.

'I think so. I think this is the kind of place they would want to spend a lot of time.'

Rick looked around with a big smile on his face.

Soon he left me and went for a walk around the hill. I started picking the flowers I didn't already have. My heart jumped when I saw a small shrub of Running Postman.

Rick came back with two flowers. One pink and one yellow.

'What are these called?'

'This is Goodenia,' I touched the yellow flower, 'and this is Bindweed.'

'So you know all their names?'

'Pretty much.'

He walked around and started asking me what individual species were called. As soon as I identified one, he pointed to the next.

'Some names are so obvious and some are so weird,' Rick said.

'Just like people,' I said, and Rick nodded.

Rick lifted the Bindweed closer to his face.

'You're right. Something so pretty shouldn't be called a weed.'

I lifted my palms in the air as if to say I told you so, but said nothing.

'My wife would like the pink one, I think. Pink was her favourite colour.'

'And my sister would love this yellow Goodenia.'

'Great,' Rick said.

I said, 'Come to my place tonight. We'll have dinner. I think my mother is making cheese and spinach pita. I could show you how to put the flowers in my flower book.'

'Sure Faruk, I'd like that,' Rick said and smiled. He winked at me and offered me the water bottle.

I smiled too and then took a long thirsty swig.

SOUL TO SELL

I came back from the park to find myself a hammer. My dad had two or three different ones in his toolbox somewhere in the shed. First, I went inside the house to see what he was doing. He was sitting in the living room staring at the wall and humming an old Communist party song. Something about young factory workers and healthy peasant girls. There was a time when if you heard him sing these songs you'd know he was in a good mood. Nowadays he was just moody.

When he saw me enter there was no hello.

'What are you looking at?' I asked, but he turned his head back to the wall and kept staring.

I went to the shed where I picked the claw hammer with a slender neck and rubber grip handle. I swung it through the air a few times, hitting an imaginary nail. The tool that had a twofold purpose felt good in my palm but there would be no nail extraction this afternoon.

I hid the hammer behind my back, under my t-shirt and went back inside where my dad still stared and hummed. When I got close to him he smelled of dry sweat and medication. I was going to have to wash him tonight.

There was just my dad and me. We rented this old unit on Main Road West opposite Jamieson Street Park. Cars buzzed along that busy road until late in the night and then just when you thought you might get some sleep, druggies, alcos, ladies of the night and coppers started their nightly dance that often lasted until the morning. I would trade a night of nightmares for the broken sleeps I was having.

Not much worked in our unit. Doors and windows had huge gaps, there was no air-con and the fence that backed onto the laneway was barely standing.

There were four taps and one shower in the unit. One tap was in the laundry to which the washing machine was connected, one in the kitchen, two in the bathroom. Only the tap in the kitchen didn't leak. My dad would put these plastic ten litre buckets under the showerhead and in the bathtub trying to save water. Trying to save money. We had no television and would go to bed at eight at night. When we had boiled potatoes for dinner, it was a good dinner. Three nights a week I stacked shelves at Safeway. They wouldn't let me do more than a five-hour shift, as I was under eighteen. My hourly rate was a misery for the slog I was doing.

'You be careful at work, Hamzik,' my dad would say to me. 'I'd be lying next to your mother in Altona if I didn't jump off that forklift.'

My mother was buried at the cemetery in Altona. She died a few months after we arrived in Melbourne from Sarajevo. Before she died, she survived a trifecta of unfortunate events, not counting the war. There was a miscarriage at the beginning of the war, pneumonia during, and a sniper shot her in her shoulder toward the end. Then she tired of living and stayed asleep one afternoon. She was on the train and was coming back from her work in the city, where she cleaned stairways in one of the office buildings. The cleaners at the train depot in Epping found her. They thought she was asleep. And she was. It was a permanent, dreamless sleep.

Dad wished the same fate for himself every time he'd get a letter from Work Cover or the insurance company that handled his injury case.

'Those vultures, the hyenas,' he'd mutter through clenched teeth while reading them.

My dad was a history teacher back in Bosnia, but here he could only get jobs for which you needed a strong back and a pea-sized brain, or an ability to switch off. He worked in this warehouse in Sunshine, where all the workers were casual, until the forklift accident when he broke his elbow and his knee.

This joint where he worked was cowboy land. Workers broke a whole heap of rules because the bosses were always on their tails. Like stacking pallets that were too heavy for top racks and not servicing forklifts on time and properly.

One thing all the blokes did, my dad included, because they had hourly targets, was to drive the forklift inside the warehouse. On paper, this was against the rules. Inside, they were supposed to use these machines called walkie-stackers. But those were electric powered and slow.

So one day my dad was stacking a pallet full of sliced beetroot cans and when the pallet was some ten meters high, he heard a grinding noise coming from under his seat. He saw the forks above him wobble and then he jumped off. He landed awkwardly between 200-litre barrels of cleaning chemicals, but he chose the right side to jump. The pallet and the forklift crashed on the other side.

When doctors took x-rays, they couldn't believe it. One in a million, they said, to break those two things in one hit. They called them very important intersections in the body where bones, muscles, and nerves interconnect and run through. It's like blowing up the intersection of Punt Road and Swan Street, including Richmond Station, one doctor said.

That same doctor said it was a hundred times better to break a bone clean than to break one of those two places. And my dad's knee wasn't just broken. It was crushed into more than a dozen pieces. So it was replaced, like a faulty car part. Now my dad was getting used to having metal and plastic attached to his leg bones.

My dad went on worker's comp, but a few weeks later that stopped when they reviewed the footage from the cameras in the warehouse. His claim got knocked back because he took off his safety belt and jumped off the forklift before it crushed him. That, they said, was against the rules and, more importantly, he drove the forklift inside the warehouse, which was against OHS rules. My father argued he was doing what everyone else was doing because the guys who couldn't meet targets weren't given any shifts, and he had to unbuckle to save his life.

The insurance company didn't care. They sent some young girl to recite the law back to my dad and his union rep. The company offered four weeks' pay and said they would not sue him for negligence and damage of company property. They were talking about the forklift, which was promptly repaired and put back into operation. The union rep, a man who spoke our language, advised him to take the offer. It was only on the table for ten minutes.

The insurance girl came back and my dad hadn't made up his mind. She sat down and shuffled her papers. Before asking my dad whether he accepted the offer, she asked on what kind of visa we had arrived with to Australia. My dad took the offer. We had no other money coming in. Later, my dad told us how he saw the insurance girl share a drink and a smoke with the union rep and then drive off in her Mercedes 4WD.

Within weeks we were food stamp poor. Later, my dad told me he fucked up, that he should have shown his teeth to his boss from the beginning. 'I should have roughed him up in the car park after the first time he threatened me with losing my job. Do it the old-fashioned way.'

We still lived in the same unit that we'd moved into when we first came to Melbourne. We found a tabby cat prowling in the backyard. The previous owners must have left him. My dad said I could keep the cat only if I called him Lenin or Tito.

In his mind, those two were forever immortal leaders of the never-ending socialist revolution. I chose Tito.

In time Tito and I got along really well. Tito slept at the foot of my bed and he'd wake me up by sitting on my belly, or if I was sleeping on my side, by tapping my head. Tito loved drinking water from those buckets in the bathroom. He was an old and clumsy cat and would often spill them. My dad would get angry and yell that the cat was ruining his life. He threatened he would kill him.

'I don't want that cat drinking from the buckets, you hear me? We could use that water for cooking or washing. The buckets are clean, and the water's good,' he'd say.

Since he could barely move, he put me in charge of the buckets.

Three days ago, in the morning while I was checking the buckets, I found Tito in the bathtub drinking the water, so I quickly picked him up. Then, while dad was eating his breakfast, he received the letter, which stated that all employees must complete extra training in safety procedures. They would be paid overtime for training. This was because of the recent workplace incident.

My dad tore the letter to pieces, took the cereal bowl from the table and smashed it on the wall. He ranted and cursed while I emptied the buckets. Tito was back in the bathtub, his tongue under the leaking tap.

My dad walked in and closed the door behind him.

'Fucken cat,' he hissed, 'I warned you both.' He went down on his knees and grabbed Tito by the neck and threw him against the wall. When Tito fell on the floor, Dad hit him across the ribs with his crutch.

Tito jumped in the air and let out a short, screaming meow. He slammed into the door trying to escape. My dad let him out and shouted, 'Fuck off!'

I ran after Tito but couldn't catch him. I came back to the house and took the crutch out of my dad's hands. I lifted it in the air with both hands and held it above my head. My dad straightened his back and shoulders, looked me in the eyes, and nodded. Then he looked at that crutch like he once looked at a Lenin's poster. There was rapture in his eyes.

I threw the crutch in the corner of the room.

My father slumped on the sofa and said, 'You're just like me.'

I picked up the phone and the phonebook. I needed to call the council, local vet and kennels and tell them about Tito just in case someone brought him in.

'The Devil isn't listed, Hamzik, or I'd call him a long time ago and make a deal. I'd sell this thing inside me,' my dad slapped his chest with his palm, 'just to go back and show the boss my teeth.'

'You've got nothing the Devil wants,' I said and walked out.

I looked around the neighbourhood for Tito and left notes about him in the letterboxes. But I had no photo. I described him as a stripy tiger-like cat, with one white paw and a missing lower left canine tooth.

Yesterday afternoon, Tito came back. His fur was matted and white membranes came out of the corners of his eyes, nearly covering them.

He sniffed his food and had a few licks of water, purring heavily, and would not let me pet him. He slept on the floor.

I told my dad there was something wrong with him and he said we had no money to take him to the vet. I had fifty bucks saved for a rainy day, so I put Tito in a box, covered him with a blanket and walked to the vet.

The vet told me that his ribs were broken and he was most likely bleeding inside. If he wasn't treated, he was going to die slowly and painfully. It cost hundreds to fix him and ninety to put him down. I thanked the vet and paid the forty bucks consultation fee and went back home.

On my way back home, I came across this prick called Otto that goes to school with me. When Otto saw Tito in the box, he said, 'Takeaway, huh? I didn't know you had some chink blood in you, Hamzik.'

I kept walking, but he pulled me back by my collar. He hit me in the stomach. The punch winded me. Otto then put his hands in my pockets and took my ten bucks.

Otto's been at me since the day I enrolled in high school. Making fun of my accent, the food I eat, the clothes I wear. I reported him at school but no one did anything. I figured out that the teachers and principal were scared of him.

When I got home with Tito, I got a pillow, went to the backyard, wrapped him in a blanket, put the pillow on top and sat on him. I sat for a long time. Until all the movements and muffled meows were distant whisper like rustling leaves. Then I buried him. I used a tomato stake to mark his grave.

Today after school I went to Jamieson Park. Some boys were playing soccer. I asked the guys if I could join the game, and they looked at the benches next to the swings. Otto was there. He stood up and said yes. When I picked a side he joined the opposite one.

I played shit. I couldn't concentrate and Otto's team scored a couple of goals because of my mistakes in defence.

'What gives, Hamzik?' Otto said. 'Can't run. No energy. You should eat some meat, mate. Maybe roast your cat on the weekend.'

They all laughed.

Otto came near me and punched me hard on my shoulder.

'Can't run, can't play,' he said.

I walked away and sat on the bench. I watched them play. Most of the boys went to my school. Some had parents who were born in Bosnia, like me. They played well and at a fast pace. One of the boys cleared the ball off his goal line by kicking it high in the air. It was an uncontrolled kick, but it did the job. He saved the goal. The ball ended up in the bushes behind me.

'Get the fucken ball, Hamzik,' I heard Otto say.

I didn't move.

'Hurry the fuck up,' Otto growled and lifted his fist.

I went into the bushes and looked for the football. As I was moving the branches out of my face, one of them sprang back and hit me in the neck. The blood spurted. It was a fair cut. I put my hand on it and my neck throbbed. This was going to take a while to heal, I thought.

I remembered what the doctor said about knees and elbows and how they never heal properly. The ball was sitting next to a rock. I picked up the rock. It was heavy and unwieldy. Insects and worms fell off it. I needed something with a handle. I picked up the ball and threw it onto the soccer field and then went through the bushes without turning back.

I went home, checked on my dad. He was humming and staring at the wall. I asked him what he was looking at, but he gave no answer.

I walked out and got myself the claw hammer from the shed.

In the living room, I shifted the hammer from behind my back. My dad was still humming and staring at the wall.

'What are you looking at?' I repeated my question.

'The green hills above our house,' he said, and his eyes narrowed. 'The wind is bending the poplars before the coming rain.'

He closed his eyes and his head dropped to his chest as if to shield himself from the wind. Tears streaked down his cheeks.

I approached him and put my hand on his shoulder. He reeked of sweat. He couldn't lift his arm and wash himself and the armpit sweat had become unbearable. The skin on his bones loosened as he lost his arm muscles. I got the crutch off the floor and leaned it on the sofa next to him.

'I'll wash you after I come back,' I said.

'You almost never regain full movement with breaks like these. They stay with you forever,' my dad said and touched his knee.

Outside, I hid the hammer in my sleeve, holding the head in my hand. I could feel the hard flatness of the face of the hammer and the sharpness of the two claws.

In the park, the boys dispersed and Otto and a couple of his faithful mates were sitting at the benches. They were sweaty and tired. They were leaning their heads on the edges of the backrests, their faces lifted toward the sun. Their chests were heaving up and down.

No one noticed me getting close. I went down on my knees and parked myself in front of Otto. I took his knee in my left hand like it was some giant nail. Otto lifted his head. I growled and curled my lips. My canines and incisors flashed at him.

I won't be selling anything to anyone.

Ever.

Otto frowned in confusion, but my hand, which held the hammer, was already pulled back behind my head. My arm muscles stretched like a bowstring before the release.

I swung down as hard as I could.

INCISION

Every first Saturday of the month, Noah took a trip to Pentridge to collect the tapes his brother Reuben had been recording in prison. Over the last year, the visits to his brother have become a messenger service of sorts. The tapes were made for their mother. Four years ago, she was knocked down by a reversing garbage truck while she was getting the rubbish bin. Since then, she has been in a wheelchair. Reuben had been in prison for the past two years and had two more to go. Noah listened to the tapes with his mother, but while she needed to hear her son's voice, he searched for answers.

Noah woke up early, had breakfast, did his homework, and started getting ready. He put the container with two large slices of shepherd's pie on the bottom of his backpack. He had helped his mother make the pie yesterday. She wheeled herself around the kitchen and he followed her instructions. He peeled the potatoes and put them to boil. He then had to cut carrots and onion into small pieces with a knife. Their food processor had broken down some time ago and they couldn't afford a new one. His mother offered to cut the vegetables on her knees.

'Just give me the chopping block and a knife. I'll be all right,' she beckoned.

But Noah told her not to worry. He got the knife, ran his fingers along the blade, touched the pointy end; the muscles in his hands tightened instinctively, and he started chopping. When later on he took the baked pie out of the oven and the robust waft of a home-cooked meal hit his nostrils, he was pleased.

'It was your father's favourite, just like Reuben's,' his mother said while he held the dish in front of her. Her voice crackled like a slow-burning campfire.

All Noah remembered about his father was that one day he was with them and the next he was wrapped in a white shroud and buried. A few days later, they moved out of their home. What was left were a few photographs, his mother's stories and the feeling that a part of him was carved off and left behind in the dark earth.

***

Noah's mother sat in her wheelchair in the living room and flipped through junk mail. She glanced at her son occasionally while he prepared for the trip. The television was on, but the sound was off. She sighed as she put the catalogues on the coffee table. Somewhere from under the frayed throw rug that covered her legs, she fished out a ball of yarn and knitting needles. Reuben's face flashed through Noah's head at the sight.

'Don't forget a bottle of water and your pills,' she said while her hands worked the needles with astonishing speed, 'and also take twenty dollars.'

Noah went to the kitchen and opened one of the cookbooks on the pantry shelf. Inside there were two twenties. He closed the book, not touching the money. He still had twelve dollars.

He slipped into his runners, put the backpack on, and leaned in to give his mother a kiss. As he did, she held him on the shoulder with one hand. She licked the thumb on her other hand and ran it across his eyebrows. Noah let her do it. There was no point arguing.

'Handkerchief?' she asked and Noah tapped his pocket.

'Make sure you call,' she instructed.

Noah nodded and walked out. His mother rolled herself to the window and watched her son gradually pass from sight, fading away in the greyness of the street.

—❦—

Noah walked to the train station, where he took a train to Flinders Street and then from there another one to the northern suburbs. On the train, he tried to read but couldn't focus. Letters peeled off the pages and danced in front of his face. The pages would not stay still. They lifted and bent as if some invisible force was at play. He looked around to see if any of the windows were open, but they were not. His muddled mind slowly cleared as last night's pill evaporated from his body.

It was midmorning, and the train was full of commuters on their way to spend a day in the city or on the beach or at a footy game or maybe on the banks of the Yarra or wherever people who are not like him went to spend a day. He wasn't sure, but if he had to, he'd bet none of them were heading to a prison to visit a relative. While he searched the faces of the passengers, he felt his eyes burning. He darted a glance to the seat across from him and saw an old lady watching him intently. She wore a heavy black topcoat. On her chest was a Red Cross pin, around the edge of the pin were the words Women's War Work.

Noah saw the old lady's lips move, but no words reached his ears. Her index finger pointed at the badge. She watched him for some time, and this made his spine stiffen. He turned away from the old lady and stared through the window. Outside, everything blended together. The sky and the landscape were grey. Grey like the colour of my soul, his mother once said when he took her for an outing to the park. He thought then that she was talking about the winter, but today he knew she had his brother on her mind.

Reuben did a whole heap of bad things: robberies, beatings, extortions, shootings; there was also the rumour that he had killed a middle-aged man with stooped shoulders who worked in a Youth Centre on Wright Street in Albion.

Their neighbours told Noah, 'Make no mistake; if your brother did take care of that bastard, he deserved it.'

For his part, Reuben did nothing to discourage the rumours. He kept quiet but when pressed he said, 'For some sickos, the only cure is a bullet in the head.'

Even the detective who came by their house to inform them that the police had nothing to connect Reuben to the murder admitted he was happy to see that man gone. 'Good riddance to bad rubbish,' he said. Shortly after, Reuben ended up in jail anyway for assault and robbery, and Noah was put on meds.

Outside, buildings slowed down, and inside, Noah's body jerked. When the train had come to a complete stop he felt a tap on his knee. It was the old lady. She offered him a biscuit, but Noah politely declined. He peeked into her bag and saw yarn and a pair of knitting needles. Just like his paternal grandmother, proud of her needlework and service in World War II.

The last time Noah saw his brother, he asked him why they called him Needle. Reuben had said it wasn't because he was as thin as a tomato stake or because he was one of those blokes who don't put their brains into gear before opening their gobs.

'You see, some people take that as needling, me talking a lot.'

'It does get a little tedious at times,' Noah countered.

'Yeah, I know. Anyway, about me being called needle,' Reuben came up so close that Noah could see the oily dirt in the cracked pores of his brother's smoke-dried face.

'Needle was my weapon of choice,' Reuben whispered. 'The knitting needle right in the neck.' He put a finger on his jugular, nodded significantly and added, 'It's messy, but quiet.'

Then Reuben did something Noah didn't expect. He took Noah's hands into his and their fingers interlocked like a cane basket. Noah felt the hardness of Reuben's finger nubs and the coarseness of his skin. He watched his brother's face. His head faintly trembled, as if his veiny neck hadn't enough strength to support the heaviness of the memories locked inside it.

'Brother, my hands are plenty filthy,' Reuben had said while still holding Noah's.

Noah pulled his hands out of Reuben's grip and placed them, palms up, on the edge of the table. He looked at them while he waited for Reuben to finish his story, but the bell rang and a guard came and took his brother back to the cell.

Noah thought about the whole scene while the train clacked on, running through the industrial estates of the outer northern suburbs. Spray-painted graffiti adorned the walls of the warehouses and factories. On the roof of one of the buildings, in thick black paint, was written 'Margot is a boy'. Noah watched the writing, craning his neck for a better view until it disappeared from his vision. The old lady did the same.

He continued to gaze out of the window even when the roof with the curious message was way behind him. The old lady stared into his eyes, intent on establishing contact. But Noah didn't feel like talking. He opened his book and pretended to read.

He got off at Coburg and walked to the prison. At the corner of Bell Street and Sydney Road he went to one of the telephone booths, put a twenty-cent coin in and called his mother. As he waited for her to pick up he could see her wheeling her chair to the hallway and reaching for the handset on the wall. He had suggested many times that the telephone be moved to the living room, but each time his mother refused. She said if they moved the phone, she'd never leave the room.

'I'm here Mum,' Noah said when she picked up.

'Good, the pie still in one piece?'

Noah stuck his free hand into his backpack, pulled the container out, and checked the pie.

'Yes.'

'You took your pill this morning?'

'Yes,' Noah lied.

'Good. Give your brother a kiss and a hug from me and call me on your way back. Love you, son.'

'Love you, Mum.'

'Don't forget the tapes.'

On the tapes, Reuben talked about his time inside, the food, the guards, other inmates, mostly innocuous gibberish so the prison authorities wouldn't confiscate them. He was able to do this on account of being a well-behaved inmate.

Their mother had said, 'You just record them, Reuben; anything at all, dear, and I will listen.'

So Reuben did. When he had nothing to say, he would read chapters from books or just sing. He would sing in English or songs in their mother's native tongue and she would listen to everything over and over again.

'Listen to his voice,' she'd say. 'He sounds very handsome. Next time, you make sure you bring me a photo of him. He sounds bigger; did he bulk up? Does he eat the food we send him?'

Only once on the tapes, Reuben had talked about his life before the prison.

'When I came back from the Army,' Reuben said, 'I got entangled with a bad crew.' But then the tape stopped and was silent for a couple of minutes. Noah always wondered who erased it. Was it Reuben or the prison authorities? He wanted to think it was Reuben.

'Noah, are you there?' his mother's voice came from the receiver.

'Yes, I'm still here. I'll bring the tapes.'

Noah cast his eyes around the booth, reading the scribbles while still holding the handset. There was a phone number and a message where to meet if one wanted to have a good time with a well-endowed man. Noah was disappointed. The message wasn't as intriguing as the one he had seen earlier on the roof of the warehouse. He turned around in the booth and started to walk out, when he saw the old lady from the train. She had one of those shopping trolleys on wheels that old folk sometimes used as a walking frame. He couldn't remember her having it when they were on the train.

The old lady had a hand-knitted beanie on her head, pulled all the way down to her eyes and over her ears. In her hand she held the book he had been reading on the train. She handed it to him. Noah took the book and thanked her.

She motioned at the telephone and her lips parted, but Noah couldn't understand her. He just said yes and held the door open while she got inside.

Noah headed for the prison. He walked the short distance, unconsciously grinding his teeth. Thoughts throbbed in his head. He stopped, had a drink of water, turned around and looked at the booth. The old lady was gone.

When he had passed the security checks, Noah was ushered into the visitor's area. There, he signed the visitor's book and got the white lanyard with a white visitor's pass. The prison officer who handed him the pass winked at him and pointed at the container.

'Apple pie again?'

'No, shepherd's.' Noah opened the container. With a long thin wooden stick, the officer stabbed the pie a few times. He then smelled the stick and gave it a lick.

'This is good. If your brother doesn't finish this, you call me.'

'Sure thing, but I doubt it.' Noah had spoken to this same officer at least a dozen times, but he couldn't remember his name.

'How's school, son?' The officer put on a serious face.

'Good. No problems.'

'Reuben said Melbourne University already made you an offer.'

'Yes.'

'That's good, son. Glad to hear it. Just keep yourself busy and you'll be right.'

'Thank you.'

'Your brother's very proud of you.'

Noah smiled and nodded.

He sat at one of the small round tables in the corner of the visitor's hall. When he saw Reuben coming, he remembered the name of the officer — Mr. Carlyle. As they hugged, Noah smelled morning breath on his brother. Reuben sat down with a thud and rubbed his face hard and long, wiping crusted drool off his chin.

'You just got up?' Noah asked.

'Something like that,' Reuben said, and launched into the pie with his fingers.

When he was finished, he wiped his mouth with his sleeve and emptied the small juice pack in one long gulp.

'Mum wants a photo.' Noah broke the silence.

'I can't mate, look at me. I look forty. Don't want to scare her.'

The brothers sat in silence. After a time, Noah spoke.

'Last time, you said they call you Needle.'

'Yes, they do.' Reuben tapped a cigarette on the table. 'You know, I could recognise his voice in a crowd of thousands. It was raspy and slimy at the same time. He smoked Lucky Strikes with no filter. There was this smell about him.'

Noah stiffened at the unexpected words as tobacco stench enveloped him.

'They moved him after complaints started flying. I kept going from church to church, pretending to want a confession.'

'Why the churches?' Noah asked.

'He was a priest.'

'The man from the Youth Centre?'

'Yeah, the same man. You remember him, right? You tutored maths to other kids there.'

'I remember going there,' Noah said, detached. The image of a hairy round belly and thick thighs appeared in front of him and he shook his head to rid himself of it. 'Then one of your mates left a message for you with me. He said the man you were looking for was in Dandenong.'

'What else?' Reuben's eyes widened. 'Do you remember?'

'I found him in Dandenong,' Noah said. 'And I made him dead.'

'Those mesh partitions in confessionals came in handy.' Reuben made a stabbing motion with his hand. He clamped his teeth and a small snorting sound came out of his nose.

Noah closed his eyes and he could see his hand holding his mother's knitting needle and the pulsating vein on the neck just above the white collar. The words were spoken in a hushed voice. The priest leant closer and said he couldn't hear it. He didn't know the whisper was about to bring a blood storm. As the blood trickled down the back of his eyelids, Noah felt his brother's hand on his.

'Are you all right, mate? Stay here, I'll get you some water.' Reuben got up and walked over to the water fountain. Noah watched his brother moving left and right in a funny, uncoordinated way. He looked like a drunken donkey on roller-skates going down the stairs, and Noah cracked a smile at that image flickering in his head. He smiled involuntarily while the thoughts born of nightmare came back and flooded his brain. The memory of being on his knees burnt his skin anew.

Reuben came back with a cup of water and saw his brother smiling. He smiled back. A bell rang, signaling the end of the visit time. Reuben held Noah by his shoulders.

'Remember my tenth birthday when Mum got me this green ice cream cake?'

'No, I don't. I was four.'

A prison officer approached them, and Reuben hurried.

'Anyway, Mum ordered this ice cream cake, and she went to pick it up in her old Corolla. It was almost forty degrees outside. She brought back this melted sludge, but we still ate it. That night, you threw up all that green mess. Mum went to work; she was packing shelves at Woolies at the time. She told me to keep giving you chamomile tea and to keep you hydrated. We slept together that night.'

'I think I remember that. You put that stuffed elephant toy I loved between us.'

'Yes!' Reuben almost yelled. The prison officer held Reuben by his arm, slowly dragging him away. 'That's right. I took real good care of you.'

'I know you did.' Noah hugged his brother and kissed him on the cheek.

The prison officer jerked Reuben a little and said, 'It's time, mate.'

They were separated and Noah felt like he was being cut. Only this time, he didn't feel wounded.

ALL THE WRONG THINGS

My father said our new neighbour looked like a bad apple and my mother let her eyebrows say what she wouldn't allow her mouth to utter.

It was Saturday, breakfast time. A van dropped off a young Aboriginal man with straight shoulders and bright chestnut eyes in front of the house on our right. He moved in with only a couple of duffle bags and a few boxes. I saw books and magazines in one, and a toaster and electric kettle in the other. An orange dog with white paws trotted after him.

'Didn't think I'd see his kind in our street.' A mix of anger and fear coloured my father's voice. 'Us Yugos and the Greeks, we're vanishing. Now with these two mongrels here,' he gestured with his thumb over his shoulder, 'the street is a bloody rainbow nation.'

That was when my mother's eyebrows started their dance. Her nostrils widened and half a snort escaped. My father craned his neck left and right, looking out the window.

'What's he looking our way for?' His eyes popped out like someone was after him.

My mother said, 'Esma, let's say g'day to our new neighbour before Alice comes.'

Alice, my school friend, helped me get an interview for a part-time job in Safeway on Main Road West where her brother-in-law was the assistant manager. I had to be at the store at midday.

'You're going to talk to that darkie?' my father spat out. 'Aren't you scared for our daughter's safety?'

'You're scared of all the wrong things,' my mother said as we stepped out.

Our new neighbour's name was Joe, and he was from a community called Eden, somewhere up north in red dirt country.

'Where I'm from,' Joe said, 'there are only two colours; red under your feet and blue above your head. And there's black, of course.' Joe ran his palm along his forearm and looked at our house.

He then stuck two fingers in his mouth and whistled, bringing his dog out from somewhere behind the house.

'This is Kanji. He almost never barks,' Joe said.

Kanji was tall and slender with a broad head that stood on his strong neck, which was nearly as thick as his hindquarters. He came to us ambling carefully and gently sniffed our outstretched hands. He lifted his head and his brown, ancient eyes observed us intently. He then turned swiftly on his big paws and walked away. His tail curved high over his back. He stopped under the apricot tree, where he sniffed the ground and walked in tight circles, readying himself to lie down. Before he assumed a resting position, something alerted him. Kanji looked up, lifting his muzzle in the air, his lean muscles stretching his shiny orange coat.

'He's never been in the city. Too much of everything at the same time,' Joe said.

'Put him on a leash or in the shed tonight. Saturday nights can get wild in our street,' my mother said.

Hook Street was long, flat, wide and straight, and because of this the hoons came in their souped-up Falcons and Commodores, tyres burning the bitumen, beer cans flying through the open windows. The residents complained to the council. Not just about the noise and lack of sleep, but about their children being scared and their pets bolting in terror into the night. The police were called regularly. There was talk about putting speed bumps on the street, but nothing came of it. In the morning, the street would be covered with burnouts, vomit, urine, fast-food wrappers, and bottles of grog.

'I've seen the burnout marks,' Joe said, and my mother and I nodded.

When we came back to the house my father rushed at us. 'That's a one hundred percent pure dingo.' His voice was full of conviction, as if he was brought up in the outback and not in the concrete jungle of communist flats in Yugoslavia.

'His name is Kanji,' I said.

'Kanji!' My father let out a scream, but the ring of the telephone cut him short.

It was my aunt Farah. We talked a little, and then she asked to speak with my father. She said, 'Girl, is your father home?' Aunt Farah said the word girl like that was my name.

My father was expecting the call. A couple of months ago, Aunt Farah had lost her job and was having money troubles, had to sell her car, and couldn't make repayments on her home loan.

Brother and sister talked for a minute and at the end, through his clenched teeth, my father said, 'I'll let you know.'

When he hung up, he yelled, 'She's moving to Sydney, wants to drop off something for Esma before she leaves.'

'You know my answer,' my mother said from the kitchen.

———

At eleven, Alice came to my house and she and my mother helped me with my outfit for the interview. My mother picked a light purple boat-neck top with a baby blue jacket and knee-length skirt. She arranged my hair in a bun and let me wear make-up. She said the outfit's colours went with my blue eyes, blonde hair and red lips. Alice held my hand and said I looked gorgeous. She ran her fingers along the collar of my top, touching the exposed skin of my neck and collarbone.

My mother smiled. 'You both look gorgeous. A long-haired blonde and a pixie-cut brunette. A perfect combination.'

Alice warned me about her brother-in-law. 'He's a perv,' she said.

At the interview, he only asked me if I had a problem handling pork products. I told him I had applied for a position in the grocery department, not the deli. He said that he'd transfer me as soon as he could. I remained quiet and stared back at him. I did my own version of the eyebrow dance. After a minute, he sighed deeply, stood up and moved to the corner of his desk. He was half a metre away from me and his head hovered over mine.

He leaned in, put on a conspiratorial face and whispered, 'I'm short-staffed in the deli. Frankly, I'm desperate. It's a fairly hard slog in there, cutting all those salamis and making sure the fish is tucked into ice. I'll give you two dollars extra per hour, but not a word to anyone. Not even Alice. What do you think?' He extended his hand.

'I have no secrets from Alice,' I said, leaving his arm hanging in the air.

'I figured,' he said. 'I'll make sure she gets a pay rise too.'

I accepted his hand, and we shook on it. When I was about to pull out of the handshake, he put his other hand on top of my hand and clasped it. He stopped shaking the hand, and then stretched his thin lips, which revealed his gapped teeth. I freed my hand when his touch became uncomfortable and thanked him for giving me the job. He said no problems, and stuck his hands into his pants, resting his thumbs on his belt.

Alice waited for me outside the store. I told her everything.

'That arsehole. You want me to sort him out?' Alice asked with a frown on her face. I shook my head.

Alice had a shift starting at one o'clock, so we agreed to meet up the next day to celebrate. She kissed me on the cheek before I left.

—⁂—

Sunday afternoon, I was getting ready to meet Alice when I heard my father's voice coming from outside. I peeked through the window and saw him talking to Joe.

'His mutt took off last night,' my father said when he walked back into the house. 'Wants us to keep an eye out.'

Outside, I told Joe I could help him put up missing dog posters when I returned.

'I don't have any photos of him.' Joe looked at the sky and then at me. 'He'll find his way back,' he said.

—⁂—

When Alice and I returned to my house, it was almost fully dark. My father came into my room. I told him about my new job and Alice's pay rise. His eyes were fixed on Alice's. She endured my father's stare before peeping beyond his burning gaze. Then her body trembled, and she stood up.

'It's getting dark. Better be on my way,' she said.

'Your friend looks like a boy,' my father said during dinner and then added that Alice looked like she was trouble. He referred to Alice in the same cold, angry voice he used when referring to my Aunt Farah. There was wild fear in his eyes, just like yesterday when he saw Joe.

While my mother and I ate, he kept tapping his tablespoon on the side of the soup bowl. A few times, he lifted the spoon and opened his mouth, but he stopped short of swallowing.

'I don't want Farah and her kind disturbing this household,' he said through his teeth, his fists clenched and resting on the table on either side of his bowl.

My mother put her index finger on her lips and said, 'Eat. The soup is getting cold.'

He brought the spoon to his mouth, only to drop it in the bowl. The hiss came out of his serpent mouth, 'She's unwed.'

On the few occasions we visited my aunt, we saw signs of the other woman living in the house. During those visits, Aunt Farah would ask my parents about swimming classes, learning to ride a bike or taking karate lessons instead of my dance classes. My parents would insist that she stop calling me girl and call me Esma. She would just wave them off and say, 'It doesn't suit her. She's no Esma.' She would deflect my parents' protestations by taking me out on the pretext of going for an ice cream, but instead she let me drive her car.

While I struggled with the clutch and the accelerator causing the car to bunny hop, she'd put her hand on my hand, manoeu-vring the gearstick, giving me instructions.

'First, the important things needed for survival. Swimming, driving, self-defence, knowing how to spot a prick,' she told me once. 'Forget dancing. Dancing won't help you if someone jumps you in the middle of the night.'

'Not planning on walking by myself in the middle of the night.'

Aunt Farah put her hands on my cheeks. Her lips formed into a line. 'Girl, they don't care about the time of the day. It's your job to be ready.'

When we returned from the drive, she always made me stand next to the doorframe in the kitchen, where she marked my height. It was part of this doorframe she wanted to give me before leaving for Sydney.

As we ate in silence, I thought about Alice. Yesterday, after my job interview, we bought a large strawberry milkshake at the 7-Eleven on Station Road. We walked over to Jamieson Street Park and sat inside the plastic castle, a part of the children's play equipment.

We drank the milkshake from the same straw and talked about things we would buy and concerts we wanted to go to. Alice took my hand, and I felt my heart go calm and my breathing slow down. She leaned over and very tenderly wiped a line of foam from my top lip. I took both her hands, brought them to my lips and kissed them. Alice pulled me into her embrace, our faces nearly touching. I stroked her hair, her cheeks, and our lips joined in our first kiss.

Afterwards, we put our heads through the small windows of the castle. Tiny, cold droplets of rain pricked our warm faces. We watched the tall, skeletal gum trees dotting the edge of the footpath in pairs, their branches touching. Behind one of the trees, an orange dog with white paws appeared.

I asked Alice to whistle.

WASPS

A bunch of us got canned from a warehouse joint in Laverton. Mostly pick-and-packers and forklift drivers. Management stayed intact. I came home with a shopping bag filled with things from my locker, a couple of coffee cups, a pair of safety work gloves, some documents and my lunch box. Twenty years in one bag. In the hallway I looked at myself in the mirror and for the first time in many years I got scared.

That was six months ago. I don't know where the time went. I kept in touch with some fellows from work for a while. I stopped when I saw two of them went for the same job as me. It was mutual. We were competition now.

A month before getting canned, I bought this ramshackle house on a huge block and moved in. Apart from my ute it was the only thing I ever bought that had some real value. Now my ute is getting old.

I was in my driveway checking a small crack in the windshield when I spotted a girl shoving a piece of paper in my letterbox. I called after her. I said a loud 'Hey.' Twice. She stopped and came back. I asked her if she could read. I knew what she was and I wasn't in the mood for her nonsense.

'Yes, I can read,' the girl said and crossed her arms over her chest. She had flyers in both hands. She could have been fourteen or twenty, I couldn't tell. She had light freckles on her nose and cheeks, and curly brown hair tied up in a ponytail. She was in shorts and a t-shirt and wore a backpack strapped across her shoulders. Not a school backpack, but something large and black. She had sports shoes on.

'Well,' I said curtly, 'what does the sticker on my letterbox say?'

Not moving a muscle she said, 'There's no sticker on your letterbox.'

I quickly walked over to my letterbox and stuck my face in front of it.

'It's the bloody kids. Little shits. They must have peeled it off. There was one of those *No Junk Mail* stickers right there.' I tapped the letterbox door, 'Just yesterday.'

The girl just nodded. Her lips formed into a line of disbelief.

'I'm not interested in whatever you're peddling.' I pulled the flyer out of my letterbox. 'You people walking the suburbs, sticking rubbish into letterboxes, I consider you people the pests.' I handed the flyer to her.

'Have a good day,' the girl said, her face flat as she spun around on her feet.

I watched her as she went from house to house until she turned the corner. I went back to my car. I looked at the windshield again and ran my finger across the tiny crevice in the glass. The more I drove the bigger the crack got. I had only a couple of grand left from my miserly payout and could not afford to fix this until I found some work. Two weeks ago I had to fork out 200 bucks to renew my forklift licence. Last week I expected to hear from a warehouse in Footscray, but no one called.

The crack had to be fixed. The coppers would not hesitate giving me a fine for it. All this trouble was because of my waste-of-space neighbour. A dropkick. It was his fault. He gives his dog roo bones to chew. One day I saw this big raven circle above my house and then dive onto my neighbour's chimney like a German Stuka plane. Except there was no screaming sound, just a gentle flap of the wings, its feathers producing a soft sound like silk rustling.

There, on the chimney, this raven, as black as blindness, perched itself and started complaining. He flapped his wings while he screeched. Maybe he was trying to scare the dog. He then dived in and I lost him behind the fence.

The next thing I saw was this big raven fly away with a bone in his beak. But the bone was too big and the bird dropped it right on my windshield. But how can I prove this? No one would believe me. So I left it alone. I said nothing to my neighbour. I stopped talking to him and started giving him the look. I think I heard him call me a wanker under his breath not that long ago.

As I was considering my options with the windscreen I saw the girl on the other side of the street. She glanced at me and our eyes connected for a second. Again, I noticed no expression on her features. I yelled after her again. This time she didn't stop. I ran across the street and apologised to her. She turned her head and said, 'That's all right.' She kept walking.

'I'll take a flyer, please.'

She stopped, turned toward me and handed me a flyer. It was about some pest control business.

'We do everything — rodents, termites, cockroaches, rabbits,' the girl said. 'Everything, except walkers. We don't do walkers.'

'Walkers?' I said.

The girl lifted her palms up and down next to her body in a look-at-me motion. I apologised again and she said that's all right again.

'I've got a wasps' nest at the back, I think.'

'I can take a look and give you a quote, if you like,' she said.

'You?'

'It's my father's business. I learnt the trade on the job.'

'You're the pest control girl.' I was surprised.

'I can drive too,' she countered. 'Or I can call my dad. He's only couple of blocks away. Walking.'

'No, no, I trust you.'

She lifted her eyebrows and shook her head. I decided not say sorry again. There was no point.

'The house or a tree?' the girl asked as we walked past my car.

'What?'

'The nest, is it on the house or on a tree?'

'Under the eaves, back wall,' I said.

We walked past my ute and the girl stopped and pointed at the tyres. 'I can't say I've seen them balder than this.'

I had a look at the tyres. There was hardly any tread left.

When we reached the backyard the girl took off her backpack. Her t-shirt was soaked wet on her back. She asked me for a glass of water and when I returned she had a new t-shirt on. She stood on one of the plastic garden chairs. I offered to bring her a ladder but she jumped off.

She pointed at the nest. 'Mud wasps, nothing to worry about and nothing we can do about, I'm afraid.'

'Why not?'

'They're not pests.'

I looked at the nest. It was round and it frightened me a little. Who knew what lay walled up in there? I'd seen these wasps fly around my garden. Droning in and out of their nest. Disappearing inside through perfectly round holes. Finding comfort in the darkness. They always looked busy, their legs dangling in the air as they buzzed from trees and flowers and back to their home.

'How long has it been up there?' the girl asked.

'It was there when I bought the house seven months ago.'

'So they've been living here longer than you.'

'Yes, but not for much longer. Their time is up. How much?' I asked her even though I knew there was no way I'd be hiring anyone for this job. I'd already made up my mind what to do. Hit it hard with a shovel. Stick the nest in a bucket full of water. The girl ignored my question.

'They're harmless and quite useful. They hunt redbacks among other things.'

The girl cast her eyes around my backyard. The grass was knee high and weeds climbed up the fence.

'You're sure to have some out there,' she said.

I looked at my backyard and said nothing in return.

She walked over to one of the rose bushes that still had some life and took a couple of petals. She squeezed them between her fingers and climbed back on the chair. She extended her arm toward the nest. Shortly, a wasp came out and landed on her palm.

'See, they're friendly,' the girl said, 'very delicate.'

I stood there watching her play with the wasp, waiting for the sting, but nothing happened. She even touched the abdomen of the wasp and the wasp dropped its wings as if to give space to her fingertip.

'I want them gone regardless. I don't like the way the back wall looks plus I'll be painting the house soon.' This was a lie.

The girl kept holding this wasp on her palm. They both looked at me, the girl with her big brown eyes and the wasp with its big black alien eyes. I could see the antennae and mandibles moving. Sun gleamed on the slender body.

'I'm afraid they'll sting.' I finally admitted. 'I want them gone. How much?'

'You're gonna have to do it yourself,' the girl said and wished me luck. I watched her leave. When she was half way down my driveway she turned. 'The nest is full of young wasps.' She stood there waiting for me to say something.

'Isn't it a school day?' I asked her.

'As much as it is a work day,' she snorted at me.

⸙

That afternoon I parked myself on the old rocking chair the previous owners had left on the back porch. I had to be careful where I put my feet and chair. The porch slats were rotted. They would have to be replaced soon. I was afraid to peer under the porch to check the stumps. I wondered if buying this old house was worth it. There was no point losing any sleep about my decision. This house was all I could afford.

I got myself a glass of milk and started watching the wasps. There was a small crack on the side of their nest. I watched their dainty orange-striped bodies drone all the way to the back fence and come back carrying small dark lumps of earth. They worked hard on fixing that crack. Their flight path was curious. They would fly straight to the middle of the fence but on the way back they would veer off to the left and as far as I could see, they flew to the side of the garage. I got up and went to the garage. There I saw an upturned rusty hubcap. A small pool of water had collected inside it. The wasps had a little rest and a drink before continuing.

I returned to my rocking chair and kept marvelling at these busy flyers. Soon I dozed off. The buzzing around my head woke me up. It was a wasp. I instinctively went to wave it off but my hand didn't move. Right on my wrist was a redback spider. Before my brain kicked into a gear and decided what to do, this wasp that woke me a moment ago zipped past my face. I never knew they could fly that fast. The wasp grabbed the spider with its skinny legs and stung him. I saw the stinger come out from the rear, pointy end of the abdomen. I also noticed that the thorax and the abdomen were connected with an impossibly thin thread. The wasp looked fragile and dangerous at the same time. It flew off to the nest with the limp spider between its legs.

I got up and washed my face under the garden tap. I checked my hand. There was no bite. I went to the shed and fished out the whipper snipper. The tank was empty. With a Stanley knife I cut a piece of the garden hose. While I sucked on the hose trying to siphon some petrol out of my ute I realised I had no feed line.

I looked at the jungle in the backyard. I pulled up my sleeves and went to work. With my bare hands I attacked the grass and the weeds. I worked until the sun was low on horizon. It was a battle. The grass and the weeds wouldn't yield and I had to pull them from the ground. Chunks of clay flew around me, hitting my face. Tiny rocks landed in my mouth. The earth got stuck under my fingernails. My hands got scratched and my back hurt.

Exhausted, I slumped down on my knees. Sweat drops ran down my cheeks and neck. My throat was parched and my temples throbbed. The veins on my neck pounded fast filling my ears with rhythmical thuds. I looked at my palms and they were bloody. Burrs and thistle stuck to my pants. My vision briefly blurred. I sat there for a time and my faculties slowly stabilised. A familiar, soothing sound came up from behind me. A faint humming filled my ears.

HOOK STREET DOGS

When we lived on Hook Street, a Heeler lived with us. For a long time this blue-grey dog didn't have a name. I don't mean to say someone hadn't named him in the past. He was in fair shape and his coat was thick and shiny. His paws were clean of wounds and his jaw full of teeth so we concluded he must've had an owner. What I'm saying is, for quite some time we didn't call him anything but Dog.

And then, not long after my paternal grandfather moved to the hereafter — his words when someone died — we found nearly a thousand bucks stashed in a small coffee can in one of his gumboots he wore when he worked in the garden. He must've known he was about to 'move' because he told my brother Isah he wouldn't be needing his gumboots anymore and he could sell them at the car boot sale in Laverton. The next morning my brother found him on the toilet seat still holding the newspaper. His bald head slumped almost to his belly button as if only held by the skin of the neck. This money paid for our school fees, a second-hand fridge and a television with a rabbit's ears antenna a little bigger than my school backpack.

The first thing we watched on the tellie was a rerun of Mad Max 2. My sisters Alma and Elma were too young for the movie. I was right on the precipice of being able to watch and my brother Isah, or Ike as he liked to be called then, was old enough to watch. Isah never liked being named after Jesus, saying that the expectation for anyone carrying the name of the prophet was too great. Within a few weeks of us landing in Melbourne, he adopted this new nickname.

My parents were too excited to stop us from watching the movie. Tyres screeching through the outback and flickering lights of the television screen impeded their parental instincts, which risked awkward questions from us, and later that night caused a nightmare for one of my sisters. I can't remember anymore which one. They were born less than a year apart, but looked like two halves of an apple.

As we watched the action Dog was curled up at our feet. Short, barely audible whines, just like my maternal grandmother's lungs would make in a few months time, kept coming out of his throat and I stroked his head and ears trying to reassure him. The heeler in the movie was called Max and when this dog appeared on the screen, our Dog jumped to his feet and barked at the television. With his muzzle he slobbered the screen, sniffing the dog in the movie. Since that night we called the heeler Max. At first I wasn't happy with the name. I wanted to call him Pujdo or Garov, the names we used to give to dogs back in Sarajevo, but everyone else seemed to like the name, so I accepted it too.

In St Albans, Hook Street was known as the kennel. Out of twenty-four houses, twenty-two had at least one dog. You could see all kinds of dogs pacing the fenced front yards or hear them barking and growling in the backyards. But mostly they were pitbulls or staffies, short, hard-muscled, thick skulled dogs with pointy little ears and grinning faces. Dogs who don't let go once their jaws lock.

Hook Street was a wide, straight street, with hardly any trees on it. As children, we thought the street was named after Captain Hook. Why would anyone call a straight as an arrow stretch of bitumen Hook Street? Two other streets vertical to Hook Street were called Peter Street and Wendy Street. There was no way in our pre-puberty minds this was a coincidence. There was a council bureaucrat out there who, in his own little way, gave the children of that corner of St Albans a little magic. The fact that a dog we ended up naming Max came to live with us was also shrouded in, well, maybe not quite magic, but a mystery for sure.

The first time we saw him was on the day we came to live on Hook Street. Max stood next to the dying apricot tree in our new backyard. Ten members of my family turned up in two cars. My dad drove a rented van with all our stuff in it. I was with him. The other car was a minibus taxi for the rest of the family. The furniture that we got for free from the Anglican Church shop on Brunswick Street in Fitzroy didn't come with us. We could not afford the proper removal truck so we gave it back.

We must have spent a good hour bringing boxes inside, looking around our new house, deciding on sleeping arrangements, making sure the lights and the stove were working and the water was running, before we ventured into the backyard.

A compact, grey-blue dog, with a dark patch around his left eye, stood still as a sprinter before the gun goes off. But Max wasn't going anywhere. He was tied up to the tree. His bright eyes considered a bunch of humans watching him. He barked loudly once as if to say he approved of what he saw, or maybe he was asking us to untie him. To this day, I'd like to think he was annoyed that it took us so long to discover him there.

My mum figured it was the previous owners who left him but my dad wasn't so sure. He said Max looked like a present someone left for us. Later we asked the neighbours about Max, but no one knew anything for sure except to say that nearly every house in St Albans had a dog and that we'd do the smart thing if we kept him.

Our neighbour on the left was an old fellow called Kevin, the only skip in our street and, according to street chatter, an ex-policeman. He told us heelers like Max weren't good in patrolling the yard but it was wiser to have a dog than not. Kevin had two dogs. A pure Rottweiler, a massive black beast, called Doc and a small sausage dog called Sam. Kevin said that with dogs you never knew. When his house was broken into, he said, it was Sam and his short high-pitched yaps, some annoying squeak a person could not call a bark, which spooked the crook. Kevin also said we picked a good name for our new dog.

Another old man called Eddy lived across the street from us and he was one of the two houses that didn't have a dog. When his sausage type dog died from eating spoiled beef sausages, Eddy decided not to get another dog. He reckoned, at eighty-six years old, any dog would outlive him and there would be no one to take care of the mutt.

Eddy's house was a carbon copy of our house. A dull weatherboard shack with a corrugated, grey tin roof. When we moved in, my paternal grandfather said the house would be enough for sleeping, eating and shitting, but he was wrong. The ten of us could barely fit.

There were my four grandparents, my parents, my brother and my two sisters. The house had three bedrooms, a living room, kitchen, and bathroom with a shower, a separate toilet, laundry and a room, which we called the sunny room. Not because it was spacious and bright but because whoever lived in the house before us had at one point intended to build a sunroom as part of the house extension that never got finished. They must have run out of money because instead of glass walls, they nailed fibro cladding on the outside. Inside, instead of plaster, the sunny room had cardboard stapled to the wooden studs and to the ceiling joists. The smallest bedroom in the house, or bedroom number three, where my paternal grandparents slept, could only be reached through the sunny room. I slept in the sunny room on a foldout couch in between two doors.

My brother Isah, who at fifteen was three years older than me, volunteered to sleep in the shed. He wrote Ike's Place on the shed door made out of a sheet of tin using black permanent marker. An electric cable was run into the shed where we had moved a few tools into one corner and set up an old army fold-out-bed in the middle. All of Ike's clothes were on the movable clothes rack hanging on wire hangers and his socks and undies were in two boxes below. During winter nights, Ike would warm up with a few water bottles and sleep in his clothes or some old pajamas. At night Ike would let in a tiny neighbourhood dog named Sook, who was fluffy as fairy floss, to snuggle with him and keep him warm.

Our neighbour on the right was called Rob. He kept chickens and dogs and he also claimed Sook was his dog, but we soon realised Sook belonged to everyone in the street. She was more like a cat, and was sometimes even seen playing with stray cats. The story went Sook was originally Eddy's dog and he got her out of the council's shelter, spayed and micro-chipped her, not realising she was a girl. Once he figured it out, he kicked her out onto the street. Old man Eddy would not admit to this.

A few days after we moved in, this neighbour Rob called over the fence, speaking in our language. He was shirtless and covered in tattoos. One of them was a cross with crooked arms. When my paternal grandfather saw it, he called it hakenkreuz. I knew this was a German word because my grandfather spent four years in Germany working as a stableman for some fat-arsed Nazi. My ears were full of never-ending stories of him as a young soldier in the Kingdom of Yugoslavia Army, which managed to put up one whole week of fighting against Wehrmacht before the whole country capitulated. It was horses and spears against panzers, he'd shout.

He was taken to Germany as a prisoner of war and sent to be a servant on account of his passable knowledge of German. He said as far as the Nazis went, the Nazi he worked for was right up there and when Russian soldiers speared him with their bayonets, it was a very good day. My grandfather said the Russians took all the livestock and machinery and then they got drunk on German schnapps. After they chased girls, he said, and this meant soldiers raped German women. Then my mother and my paternal grandfather argued about women paying for the sins of the men, but my grandfather cut all talk short by saying all Krauts knew about the evil being done in the camps.

Rob also looked like a man who had done evil back in his younger days and the way he hissed his words, he looked like he wasn't done doing it. He held a hammer in one hand and said he knew Sook slept in the shed with Ike. He said he gave his dog the name Sook because she complained too much. Then in the same breath, he said his other dog, also a bitch, had a litter, and he was looking to offload some of the puppies at a cheap price.

My father declined telling him we already had a dog and Rob said we should come around and that Heelers were good for sheep but not for attacking burglars. He said everyone needed a good dog in this shithole and our eyes would eventually open.

Rob then disappeared for a moment behind the fence and when he came back, he lifted one of the pups by the scruff over the fence. He said the pup was a pure dobie, docked and cropped. He smacked the Dobermann pup on the butt where his tail once stood. Rob then flicked his taped ears that stood erect like two triangular sails. The pup had big bright eyes and when his snout was close to Rob's face he licked it few times.

Rob said he must be careful with the pup's ears for about six weeks. This was so they stay up. And then he said we could have the dog for fifty dollars. My father said nothing, and he put his hand on my shoulder and we went inside the house without a word. Inside, my paternal grandfather, who had listened through the open window, argued the tattooed Nazi monkey was right and we needed a proper guard dog in this shithole. He then pulled out fifty dollars somewhere from his chest and tried to give it to me, but my father stopped him saying we had a perfectly good dog.

My maternal grandparents slept in bedroom number two, my two sisters in bedroom number one, and my parents in the living room. There was no heating or air conditioning in the house, which had a tin roof. The house was once painted in white, which over time turned into grey, and then it started to flake off. It was a noisy house. I could hear my family snoring and farting and turning in squeaky beds on uneven floorboards. I could hear when my grandfather took his medicine and burped after swallowing his pills because they gave him instant gas. I could hear, but not very often, the muffled sound of my parents doing naughty stuff. There was a distinct rhythmical, sloshing sound, as if someone was sending loud air kisses. One time when my sister Alma awakened to go to the toilet, she interrupted them.

I could hear my sister asking about the noise and my mother explaining it was the neighbour's cats drinking milk on the front porch outside.

I could hear cars driving past, neighbours talking or dogs growling at shadows in the night through the buckled horizontal boards that didn't sit properly on top of each other. I could hear plants outside brushing against the wood and cats using the house as a scratching post. In late autumn, when the leaves started to turn brown and the first winter chill would whistle through the boards, the house creaked with the wind and change in temperature. Most other houses in the street were weatherboard, although some had fake brick cladding which started to separate where the panels met. They were all grey and sickly-looking thanks to smoke coming from a chemical factory in Deer Park. Even so, it was still heaps better than the housing commission flats in Atherton Gardens in Fitzroy where we came from.

There was a huge backyard, and it had a cubby house and a pear tree and a half-dead apricot tree. The grass hadn't been mowed in ages and all types of weeds fought a silent war of fauna supremacy. When I walked through it for the first time, the grass tickled my still hairless privates. When my brother Isah saw me, he yelled after me to get out of the weed jungle before a snake or a redback spider bit the little sausage between my legs. Pretty soon, we bought ourselves a second-hand sixty-dollar lawn mower from Cash Converters on Station Road. The machine conked out five minutes in its first job.

It was around this time my father lost his job in a chemical factory in Deer Park and when Rob knocked on our door and said he had to warn us about Max. He said Max was about to be stolen. He took us to the street and pointed at a blue, spray painted cross, smaller than the span of your hand from index finger to thumb, just below the letterbox, on the front fence. It looked like someone's poor attempt at graffiti vandalism or street art depending on where you stood on the matter of bored, drunk and drugged youth ruining the properties around St Albans. As far as I was concerned, graffiti in our neighbourhood had nothing to do with art. And I was glad the local coppers shared my opinion. Of course, there was no stopping these bastards. These youngsters mostly attacked train stations or warehouse walls and glass shop fronts and rarely came into suburbs. When they did come, they defaced houses and cars. It wasn't unheard of for someone's front fence or car parked on the street being spray-painted into an oblivion of loud colours and rude pictures. Except this time, it wasn't the graffiti gangs. At first, we didn't believe what Rob told us.

Rob knew this would be the case, and he said we should take a real good photo of Max before he disappears. We'd be stapling lost dog photos soon to the electric poles. Photo or no photo, Rob said, it didn't matter. No one would look twice at the dog's mug, anyway. In St Albans, mongrels like him were as common as mud. Max, Rob said, was bound to rot on landfill at Deer Park or else his mutilated body would be burned with other unlucky dogs somewhere beyond Rockbank, beyond city limits. Sometimes the crooks that ran the dog-fighting joint were too drunk and couldn't be stuffed with loading up the dead dogs at the back of their utes and dumping them on the tip. I watched as an agitated Rob paced up and down our front yard. Anger accumulated in my throat, burning my windpipe as if I swallowed a chili pepper. So much evil, so close to our doorstep. Then Rob said he had seen many dogs die in the fighting pits and he just wanted to help. He started to cry.

Isah and I went for a walk up and the down the street and we noticed some houses had the same painted blue sign on their front fences or near the letterboxes. Over the next few days, we kept Max chained in the backyard. Not long after we heard only one dog was stolen from the street, an old pitbull who lived with a woman called Gina.

Gina always had pitbulls. The first time she got herself a pitbull she went to some backyard breeder in Altona and got herself three pitbull pups, all boys. She chose them soon after they were born, but picked them up six weeks later. She was determined to create a lasting bond between herself and the male pups to prevent from being raped in her house again. I know what Gina saw when the pups were born. We had a girl dog back in Sarajevo. Her name was Lila. She had only one litter right before the war stopped the regular flow of life. I remember crouching down with my sisters and my brother watching five slimy balls fall out of the dark ring that widened under the Lila's tail. Those balls of new life squirmed for a bit on an old blanket before Lila gathered her strength and chewed off the cord and licked her tiny offspring clean.

Everything went well with Gina, and her three pitbulls for a couple of years until the dogs matured. Then she came home one day and found one dog dead, a second dog a bloody mess who had to be put down, and a third dog hid during the fight for dominance but didn't eat for a week. It was this third dog that was stolen from Gina. It didn't take long after before we saw a removal truck pull up in front of Gina's house.

The fellow who lived right next to Gina was called Rudolf and we never found out which country he was from. He kept two brown dogs with floppy ears, which were cute as buttons. People called them bird dogs because they liked chasing birds but they were in fact gundogs used for hunting ducks and wild geese. They were a dog breed that was trained from a very young age to cope with the sound of a shotgun. But they were a mix, not pure and not especially smart. Both got killed the same way, hit by a car on Hook Street, chasing magpies. One of the gundogs was luckier than the other and was hit by a minivan, instant death. It took the other nearly an hour to die because he was just kind of swiped by the side of a small car. Rudolf picked him off the street and put him on his front lawn and wailed. Then Rob walked over there and told him he should put down the dog but Rudolf couldn't bring himself to take him to the vet. He also said he had no money for the vet. Rob knelt next to the dog, examined his bleeding body and broken legs, lifted his head and broke his neck. Rudolf slapped him and threw clumps of grass and rocks at Rob as he walked away.

Gina's house stood empty for a while and just when we thought someone with money would buy it, raze it to the ground and put some units on the block of land, we heard a family would be moving in. People said they were some country folk coming to Melbourne looking for work. They had an orange farm or something near Mildura, but all that was gone. Not because of a lack of rain or suffocating dust or some other problem a man couldn't control. This happened because it became cheaper to bring oranges in ships from halfway across the world until all you could taste when you ate those oranges was anger.

In my head, after almost twenty years, their arrival is still pin-sharp clear. These country people came in an old Kingswood station wagon packed to the brim with boxes, suitcases and duffel bags. The clunker had faux wood grain paint inside and out as if drunken elves put it together. It was early July, and the temperature was in single digits. A southwestern wind blew straight from the heart of the Antarctica and brought the rain in waves.

The wagon pulled up in front of our house. I put on my jacket, stuck my head into my school beanie, slipped into my boots and walked out on the front porch where under the crooked and leaking tin roof I waited for them to come out.

If you hitched a trailer to a beat-up car, I thought, you could be forgiven for thinking you were back in Bosnia watching

Roma folk pull up. Except this was different. They would only hang around for a few days before their adventurous feet got itchy, or the bigoted locals had enough of dark-skinned people in their neighbourhoods. These country people were here to stay.

But there was no trailer. No trinkets for sale or futures to be told by a near-dead Roma oracle, either. Instead, parts of a single bed, including a mattress wrapped in see-through plastic sheet were strapped to the improvised roof rack, which was made out of planks of wood, and alu pipes. A blonde girl sat at the front, on the bench seat, squashed between two sweaty adults, probably her parents. When the doors opened, three humans and a good-sized dog spilled out of the car like coloured wax out of a broken lava lamp. The dog lifted his muzzle and took a deep whiff of his new surroundings. He barked once and then shook himself. Droplets of water flew off his hind legs. The two adults and the girl stretched their limbs and cracked their knuckles. The man wiped his face with the back of his hand. The woman straightened her shoulders and adjusted her skirt. The girl took a sip out from a water bottle.

These people were knackered. Their dog looked like our Max, with the same colour coat, but no patches. Later, the blonde girl Nina explained it was called a full mask and that Max had half a mask. Nina knew lots about animals. She said I should walk Max every day because there was working dog blood running through his veins and he couldn't help wanting to run and chase.

When the people from the car spotted me sitting on the steps of the front porch, they nodded and the girl waved. I waved back.

It took a while for me to cross paths with the new girl and her dog. It was the first week of summer holidays and all the school children from Hook, Peter and Wendy streets and a little further away from Pennell and Scott avenues gathered at the man-made lakes off Andrea Street. The ammunition factory that once stood there was torn down and a new suburb was about to spring up on the paddocks south of St Albans. But the first thing the construction people did was to dig up five huge holes and create interconnected lakes. The residents of the new suburb would have a pleasant view.

Kids brought their bikes and their towels and their dogs to the shore of the lakes. My heeler and Nina's heeler, a girl, hit it off in a flash. At one point it looked like they were kissing. But they never had any pups as Nina's dog was spayed and she said I should do the same with Max. That and the vet sticking a microchip under his skin was the responsible thing to do.

Over time, Nina's father and my father became friends. Their friendship was borne out of their predicament. One good thing about Hook Street houses was they were all on large blocks of land. Our fathers began working the land planting all sorts of produce, from potatoes and carrots, tomatoes, spring onions to four kinds of berries. On those three plots they had sixteen fruit trees, three kinds of apples, two kinds of pears, apricots, plums, peaches, nectarines. They got permission from the council to cultivate a vacant piece of land under which huge storm water pipes ran and no one was allowed to build anything. After that they started hiring a spot and a table at St Albans Market where they sold their produce.

When I drove through Hook Street last week, I saw no dogs but I knew they were there. All of my grandparents were dead and my parents lived alone. The visit was short. My mother said she had liver problems, or maybe it was her gallbladder. She clutched to her referral for an abdomen ultrasound and said she had an appointment on Friday. My father took her hand and said it would be all right. I said I would call her on the day of the ultrasound.

When I left, I drove on Main Road West and past the vet station where Nina worked as a vet. She still lived in the area. My sister Elma and Nina bought a townhouse in the new suburb they built on the paddocks where the ammunition factory once stood. They lived with two adopted cats and two adopted pit-bulls from a shelter. These dogs were rescued after police busted a dog-fighting ring somewhere near Melton. More than twenty dogs were put down at Nina's vet station, many of them by her own hand. The two that were given a chance were barely out of the puppyhood stage. They cowered every time someone raised their voice or hand.

My mother said the last time she went over there for a visit, she told them both taking care of dogs is all well and good, but the next creature in their family should be a human baby. I drove past the vet station and wondered if I had time to go to the little hill near the man-made lakes. Isah and I buried Max there in the middle of the night some years ago. Max lived with us for twelve years. He was a mature dog when we found him all those years ago in our backyard, so he lived a long and good life for a dog. I remembered the first time Nina and I spoke. She said Heelers are hardy dogs suited for the harsh climate of our dry continent and we could learn so much from them. I don't know if I learnt anything from Max. I never saw him jump on a cow's back or nip at their heels. When we found him, he wasn't a working dog anymore and I am not sure he ever was. A couple of times a year Max, Isah and I would track the length of Kororoit Creek Trail from Sunshine to Ardeer and it was then I saw how tough Max was. He could go all day on a few licks of water and one meal in the morning. He never ran, but rather trotted, and always with his tongue rolled up in his mouth, finding a shaded spot for a rest every hour or so. A few times we got lost, but Max always brought us back to the right path.

As the flatness and grayness of St Albans receded in my rear-view mirror I began to think some of Max' inborn toughness rubbed off on me and Nina's words might be true for me as well.

DINOSAUR

Sam pissed on the horse sculpture I made out of a block of ice. He took the sculpture out of the warehouse, put it on the drainage gutters in the loading dock, fished out his prick, letting his nutsack hang out, and let it spray. The blokes in the cold storage cackled like a bunch of witches. Sam's been a bastard from day dot. Every place has one.

A month ago I got the forklift job in this warehouse joint, Carl's Cash'n'Carry, a wholesale business where everything is sold in bulk. You can buy thousands of this and five tonnes of that. Crap like three kilo cans of pineapple rings or HB-grade lead pencils in boxes of hundred. All shrink-wrapped and sold on pallets. I don't know of anyone out there who could carry a loaded pallet. I haven't seen the Hulk doing his shopping here. You had to come with a truck.

It was mid-December, hot and slimy, and the condenser pump in one of the walk-in freezers conked out. It happened right after Friday morning's group meeting. Carl, the owner, addressed the anxious, short-tempered mob of about fifty workers.

He held meetings on Friday morning because Thursday afternoon is payday and this gave him a chance to start every meeting with the line, 'I hear it took a little longer for you fellows to get home last night.' At this point he always stopped, grinned like a capuchin with a hard-on, and then he'd say, 'carrying all that cash in your pockets.' He referred to our pay, that is handed to us in sealed envelopes and to the name of his company. A nice double entendre, though I doubt it was intentional. But what do I know? Carl's loaded and driving a Mercedes and I still live at home with my parents and ride to work on a bicycle.

Carl always delivered the same speech with a frothed mouth. Even priests these days made an effort to vary their sermons, but not Carl. No one else talked except Carl. Sometimes Penny said something about our pay, overtime, or allowances.

This morning I heard someone behind me say, 'She really let herself go.'

'Can you blame her?' the other voice replied.

Then Carl said something about the work culture at Triple C — that's what he called his company — how he expected this and that, and he wouldn't stand for this and the other thing.

Evidently, Carl expected things like stocking the freezer to the brim, making sure there's no airflow. Our supervisor told us to stock the cool rooms to the ceiling. So the combination of stupidity, disregard for regulations and heat nearly brought down the whole warehouse. We moved as much as we could into the second freezer room, but still had heaps of stuff left. Carl, a tight arse through and through, bought a truckload of ice bags and two dozen large ice blocks instead of hiring a portable cool room, while electricians tried to fix the pump.

His managerial genius was on full display at my workplace. I wondered what Carl's next move would be. Joining together in prayer for a cool change in the weather?

We covered the goods with ice and had one ice block left that we couldn't fit inside. During my lunch break, I got a Stanley knife, size 18 flat head screwdriver and a hammer and created my masterpiece. It took me about half an hour.

'This isn't your night school mate,' Sam groaned while I worked.

I'd told one person I was doing a short course in sculpting and overnight I became something different from the rest of them. That wouldn't be too bad, but I'd told Penny, the pay girl from the office. Everyone calls her fat Penny because there is another Penny in the office. Also, fat Penny is fat.

Blokes in the warehouse say things about Penny. She'd arrive at work in her little Corolla around eight and park at the side of the warehouse. Blokes made fun of how her car was lopsided on the driver's seat, how when she got out, the car sprang up like it was able to breathe again or how the wooden steps leading up to the office above the warehouse sagged under her.

'Imagine that fat arse sitting on your face,' Sam said one morning while a bunch of them watched her go upstairs.

'At least she's got tits to go with the bum,' another bloke said. 'I wouldn't mind diving in there face first.'

They talked right under the stairs as she went up, sucking on their cigarettes and drinking their sodas. Penny never said anything. Neither did I.

When I was done with my ice horse, people crowded around me, and I saw flickers of admiration in their eyes. The horse had turned out beautifully. I even chiselled out the mane and a flowing tail.

Our supervisor broke through the crowd.

'All right Michelangelo, nice job destroying company property,' he said. 'Out in the sun it goes.'

Sam volunteered his muscles and urine. After this the supervisor sent me to the non-perishable area for the rest of the day. There wasn't much for me to do, except find ways to avoid the supervisor, so I snuck out to the office to check if my safety boots had arrived. Uniform orders went through Penny.

I'd ordered a pair of steel caps a month ago when I started. The money for the boots had been deducted from my pay already. I was still without them and my supervisor was riding me real hard like it was my bloody fault. He was going to be an even bigger prick now that I'd made an ice horse.

I was eager to get the boots. I worked in regular work boots, no steel caps, and was scared a pallet or a forklift would crush my foot. I'd seen it happen. You would think in a warehouse like this, where there are dozens of pallets with safety boots sitting on the racks, you'd be able to get a pair without any dramas, but no. The boots had to be ordered from some other joint like Triple C. I didn't know what kind of scam Carl was running, but I was sure he was pocketing some of my money somewhere along the way. You didn't get rich like him by being straight.

'Leading up to Christmas, everything slows down. Deliveries, post, everything,' Penny told me.

She pulled a few tissues from the box on her desk and wiped her forehead, face, and behind her ears.

'And this heat doesn't help.' I saw sweat marks under her arms on the blouse that stretched nearly down to her hips. The fabric was caught between the rolls of fat on her stomach and it was wet, too.

'I heard about the ice horse,' she said, and I shrugged. Then she asked me for a favour.

From under her desk, she pulled out a box of plasticine and asked me if I could make a dinosaur for her son. She said he liked making things out of modelling clay, but that it didn't weather well, so she bought him plasticine. She said he would love it and that dinosaurs were his favourite.

I took a green block and modelled a long-necked dinosaur with spikes along the back and tail and drew the eyes and mouth with a pencil.

'So plasticine doesn't dry out like modelling clay?' Penny asked.

'No, it's oil based.'

'It can stay outside?'

'Sure, just make sure it's not in direct sunlight.'

She got a clear plastic zip-lock bag and carefully put in the dinosaur.

'I'll get one of those clear plastic boxes when I get home. It'll look nice. My son will love it. It was his favourite thing to play with.' Penny looked me straight in the eyes as if I knew something.

At that moment, I heard my supervisor, 'Get back to the warehouse and no more bludging.'

I wanted to ask Penny what she meant, but the supervisor took my shoulders, turned me around toward the exit and said, 'And stay away from that arse-licker, Sam.'

I left, wondering what Penny had said. When I returned to the warehouse, Sam stopped me.

'Been a while since you had a root, mate?'

'Bugger off,' I snapped.

'You wanna get yourself some of that warm chunkiness, I reckon.'

I kept walking.

'She's been on the lookout for someone to deposit a baby in her fat gut,' he yelled after me. 'She needs to move on, be a mommy again.'

Like two and two are four, things became clear in my head.

I walked back. A roar came out of my chest. My fist connected with Sam's jaw. He fell face down.

Blood spatter dotted the concrete close together, almost melting into a puddle. Sam's feet twitched and his steel caps made a tapping noise on the concrete like someone using Morse code.

GOOD BOY

Sneg was between assignments. That's how the agency referred to it. He called it being between dogs. Early Monday morning he drove to the pet supplies store at the back of the shopping centre. It was winter and daylight still chased the night away. First in, he felt like the place opened just for him. He looked at the piece of paper with his scribbles on it. He took the notes on Friday afternoon while a man from the agency spoke to him on the phone.

Agency-man's voice was heavy. He said he was in a bit of a pickle and something had come up. Something unexpected. Something unexpected always comes up, Sneg felt like saying.

One of his clients got a call from the hospital that there was a slot for the operation she had been waiting on. She had to be in hospital on Monday morning. It was one of those operations that could go either way, Agency-man sighed. Sneg pictured a large man on the other side.

Sneg agreed to take the job. He asked about the dog and Agency-man said it was a German Shepherd. There is one more thing, Agency-man huffed, the client doesn't have time to prepare all the food and meds. She's ordered the meds and they could be picked up from the pet store not far from where he lives. If he could buy the food, the agency would reimburse him after the assignment, of course.

So in the pet store Sneg looked at his scribbles. The dog, Maurice, not Morris, and not really a name for a German Shepherd, he thought, ate different brands of dry dog food and canned food. They were on opposite sides of the store. He put four large bags of dry food in the trolley. He wheeled the trolley past the toys, the sleeping mats, the plastic dog houses that looked like the first strong wind would dismantle them into pieces, the leashes and the collars. He found canned food and took ten large cans.

At the counter a young girl with jet-black hair was sitting on a tall stool, typing on the computer. She had piercings in her ears, her nose, and lips. When she opened her mouth to speak he saw she had studs along the length of her tongue. Her make-up was black. Her lips and her fingernails were black. Every item of her clothing was black. The girl had a look on her face like she was somewhere else. Or maybe she was burdened by something. He couldn't tell.

He said good morning and the girl's eyes remained glued to the screen. While he waited for a response, he checked his list and counted the bags and cans in the trolley. He said good morning again, louder this time.

'How can I help you, sir?' the girl said looking at the screen and then she said good morning.

He gave her his surname, Sneg, and told her about the medication. She bent and got the large box from under the counter. A little chiming sound came from the computer and her eyes darted back to the screen and moved rapidly while she read. Her fingers typed furiously, her eyes narrowed, and she bit her bottom lip.

While she typed he shuffled through the box and found Maurice's medication. He gave her his credit card and she rang up the sale. She looked at his card while he signed the slip.

'Your surname means snow, right?'

He nodded.

'I'm Alicia,' she chirped. The girl suddenly assumed a pleasant demeanour. Her black eyes sparkled under the heavy make-up. He wondered what colour her eyes were under the black contact lenses.

She didn't speak his language, she said, but her grandparents did and they still insisted to this day that she learn. She made a dismissing gesture with her hand.

'If I didn't learn when I was six, no way I'm gonna learn it now.' She shrugged and her eyebrows lifted in expectation, but Sneg offered no words.

'Maybe you know them. Lukovic,' she said their surname, 'from Keilor.' He said he didn't know them.

The girl spoke again, explaining who her grandparents were and that for years they had a continental deli in the shopping centre. 'You could buy any type of cured meat from the Balkans, even rabbit and goat. They used to say their sausages could cure any vegetarian,' she said jokingly.

Sneg cracked a smile. 'I don't know many people,' he said, 'but I know their dogs. If they have a dog, we might have crossed paths.'

The girl dropped her eyebrows and made a perplexed face.

'I mind dogs for other people, when they're on holidays and such. I'm retired. Gives me something to do.' He wasn't happy about the last thing he said. He didn't need to explain himself to anyone.

'Oh,' the girl, Alicia, said, 'you're a dog-sitter. That's nice.'

He preferred the word dog-minder, but said nothing. In his mind, which after more than half a century still worked on the principles of his mother tongue, a dog-sitter was someone who sits on dogs.

Sneg put the dog's medication in his pocket, touched his hat and walked out with the trolley.

***

The van pulled up in front of Sneg's house a little after three in the afternoon. Agency-man was late. Sneg stuck his right hand into the dog food bag and put a few dry biscuits in his pocket and walked out. He met the dog, Maurice, outside.

The huge black dog jumped out of the side door and shook himself on the nature strip. Agency-man had him on the leash and Sneg went down on his heels and extended his hand with his fingers curled into a fist.

Maurice sniffed his hand and gave it a good lick. With his left hand, Sneg patted his neck and offered him a biscuit. The dog wolfed it down. Sneg took the leash and unhooked it from the collar.

'Sorry about being late,' the driver said and Sneg recognised the voice from the phone. Agency-man wasn't large. Except for eyes that did not rest, he was an ordinary man of forty or so. His eyes looked too big for their sockets. A weird image flashed of the man's eyes popping out and Sneg trying to put them back in. Then the images of different body parts danced in his head.

Sneg saw his hands pressing down on a little chest, being careful not to crush the fragile rib cage. He saw his ex-wife exhaling into the boy's purple lips. He saw the boy's eyes roll up until only whites were visible. Some things you cannot un-see. They become you.

'There's no use fighting life,' his father whispered in his ear at the funeral. 'It's like expecting your hair to stay dry in the rain.'

Agency-man apologised again, and this brought Sneg back and he said, 'It's not a problem.'

'Poor woman,' Agency-man said. 'She was on the way to the hospital this morning to have her surgery and she was late. There was this huge pile-up on the Hume Highway. Huge mess. You must have heard on the news.'

Sneg shook his head.

'That's why I'm late. Her son was going to drop her off and then bring the dog to us. But then that mess happened. It was real bad. I went there to get the dog. Least I could do.

You haven't seen the news?' Agency-man asked again and Sneg shook his head again. 'Some kid threw a rock or something from the overpass and it hit one of those trucks that transport livestock. The truck was full of sheep. So this truck flips on its side, jack knives, smashes through those roadside barriers and blocks both sides of the highway. Real mess. She had to backtrack. She's in hospital now. She was told they'd slot her in first thing tomorrow morning.'

Agency-man looked at Sneg and continued. 'Bad omen, I say, all those dead sheep lying on the road. It took them a whole day to clean up the mess. I tell you it was a sight I will never forget. Out of nowhere, somewhere from under the truck, I mean no one knows, this Kelpie dog appears, right? He starts running around herding the half-crazed sheep. The bleating was deafening. He's all covered in blood. *He* was something.'

'You see, the drivers take them in the boxes under the load next to petrol tanks. What a place to be in an accident, huh? That's how they travel. So this one Kelpie, he survives somehow, it's a miracle, and he runs around like mad. His fur is bloody, his eyes wild. He looks like he slaughtered half of those dead sheep. So he starts chasing the surviving sheep. Some sheep listen to this dog and they start gathering into a mob. I tell you it was something. I will never forget it! That dog saved the clean-up crew hours. Gathering the sheep like that!'

Sneg tried to picture the scene but gave up. He'd wait for the news.

'And in the end, the poor bugger, he just drops dead. He drops dead! He lost all his blood from a cut or something. He does his job and dies. Crazy!' Agency-man was out of puff. He took a deep breath, like he was going to dive.

'I tell you some of the kids today.' He made his hand into a fist and his lips narrowed to a line. 'Sometimes they grow up to be bastards,' he said through his clenched teeth.

Sneg wondered if the news would mention the Kelpie and heard himself say, 'That is something.' He thanked the man and shook his hand. He then tapped his thigh and started for the door and Maurice followed. Over the years he learnt that being relaxed but firm worked with all dogs. It was something the dogs taught him.

On the porch he opened the door, let the dog in and lifted his right thumb up for Agency-man to see. He wasn't between dogs anymore.

Inside, he served the dog a bowl of dry dog food and a bowl of water. While Maurice ate, Sneg observed. Except for the bottom part of his legs, Maurice was otherwise all black. He was ten years old, a grandfather in terms of years for a dog that size, but he still looked imposing. At the withers, he was the length of Sneg's forearm and his paws were the size of his fists. His head was massive, and it looked like he could fit a human head in his jaws. Sneg never had a dog this size in his house. He once took care of an eight month Huskie pup, and the pup looked like he could pull a small car. But Maurice was a full-grown, mature dog whose bearing demanded attention.

Maurice was *the* dog. So was that Kelpie.

When Maurice finished his food, Sneg got his Polaroid camera. He took a photo of every dog he ever cared for and now it was Maurice's turn. The dogs became the children and the family that he should have had.

He let the dog sniff the camera and then took him into the spare room. In there, blue-tacked on the wall, were ninety-two photos. Maurice had a look at the wall and barked as if he understood Sneg took care of all his canine brethren.

Sneg ordered Maurice to sit and Maurice sat. He went to his knees and pressed the button. The flash went off and Maurice barked in protest at being blinded by it. Sneg quickly shoved a biscuit in front of his face and the dog swallowed it.

The flash in his old Polaroid camera made a small whizzing sound. The film came out, and he took it. He held it and looked at the clock in the kitchen, his eyes following the thinnest hand. After a short time, he pulled the black foil off the film and the print of Maurice appeared. His black face stood against the white of the wall and gave the print a monochrome appearance. By far it was the worst photo he had ever taken and he wondered for a minute if he should take another. He decided to give Maurice a reprieve from the flash, at least for today.

He stuck the photo on the wall. Maurice gave it an investigative sniff and barked once, in what Sneg took as approval.

The next morning, he took Maurice for a walk. When they got home, there was a card waiting in the letterbox. It was from his ex-wife. As always, it simply read 'Love'. She always signed it with her first name only and drew a small heart in a red pen. He pulled a box from his desk drawer and placed the card inside. There were forty-one cards in total. They all said the same thing.

Sneg never blamed his wife for leaving. In fact, he was relieved when she did. The boy took after her and every time he looked at her face, pain flooded him. He could not bear a lifetime of reminders of what life briefly promised, but never delivered.

He loved her and what they briefly had together too much. She deserved another life, and he was content not to have one. Death determined the path of his life and he accepted it. He often thought about his son. He consoled himself with something he heard a long time ago.

You are only really dead when everyone's forgotten about you, he had heard or read somewhere. Suddenly, thinking of that, a chill went down his spine, and a terrifying feeling shook his core. He strained his brain trying to picture his son's face. He tried and tried until his head started hurting. His brain searched his memory and the harder he tried; the harder it got to put any coherent thoughts together. It's been forty-one years. The eyes, were they blue or green? Chubby facial features melted in the fogginess of his memories. His heart raced, and he ran to his desk in the study where he kept the album. Inside there were only a dozen pictures. Fast, he flipped the pages and found the photo. The eight by ten portrait was framed by a vignette of doves holding blue and white ribbons in their beaks along the edges. The cherubic face of a happy toddler with a beaming smile stared at him. Sneg ran his fingers across the face.

'Such a good boy... you were,' he whispered.

Teardrops fell on the child's face in the photo. He suddenly had a great desire to hold the boy again, to rock him on his knee, to rub his back until he burped. The force of this desire hit him like the blast of an open furnace making him hot and dizzy.

Maurice came up from behind and sat next to him. The dog watched the photo of the boy and made small whining sounds. He put his muzzle on the photo and then into Sneg's lap.

Later in the afternoon, he went to the garage and pulled a large carton box from under the workbench. He got a Stanley knife and opened it. He got a screwdriver and a set of Allen keys. Inside there was a wooden rocking horse, still in pieces. After he put it together, Sneg and Maurice went for a drive to St. Vincent's where he left the toy.

***

On the fifth day of Maurice's stay, Sneg received a phone call from the agency. It was the same Agency-man with the heavy voice. Maurice's owner would have to stay a little longer in the hospital, he said. Things got complicated during the operation. Sneg agreed to take care of Maurice until further notice.

'How do you two get along?' Agency-man asked.

'No problems,' Sneg answered. He waited to see if Agency-man had something more to say. He was chatty the last time they spoke.

'Good to hear, good to know,' Agency-man said.

To Sneg he sounded like he had more to say but Sneg wasn't the one to ask questions he didn't want to know answers to.

They drove to the big park where dogs were allowed off the leash. It was nearly half an hour away from Sneg's house and Maurice sat quietly on the front seat, buckled up like a person, observing the world through the window. Such a well-behaved dog, Sneg thought. From experience, he knew that occasionally large dogs could give you a bit of a headache until you established yourself as a leader. The blood of the pack animal still ran deep in their veins. No such case with Maurice. He was a pleasure from the moment he jumped out of the van.

In the park, they played fetch with a frisbee and walked along the bush trail where Maurice half-heartedly gave chase to rabbits and magpies. He ran with his tongue out and he would come to Sneg for pets. He would stand up on his back paws and put his front ones on his chest while Sneg scratched his furry belly. Standing like that, they were nearly the same height. Sneg could feel the powerful muscles on the dog's chest, shoulders and legs. He had to brace himself every time Maurice jumped on him like this, putting one of his feet half a step back and bending his knees slightly for balance. He worried the weight of the happy dog would knock him down. But Maurice knew how to pace himself. It was a marvel to see such control. He would leap at Sneg with all his might and just before he connected with his chest, he would break mid-air, his paws landing softly.

That evening, after a good play in the park, they both worked up an appetite. As soon as Maurice entered the house, he positioned himself next to the food bowl. Sneg ate left over baked potatoes with a garden salad and Maurice got double his regular portion. They went to bed full-bellied.

A little before midnight, Maurice awoke. It was like he was prodded with electricity. He jumped up, pricked his ears and barked. He stood in darkness for a few moments, trying to orientate himself. Then he barked again, and again and kept barking. He quickly woke up Sneg.

'What's wrong, boy? Is someone out there?' Crusty eyed, Sneg searched for the cricket bat in the wardrobe.

Maurice's barks turned to howls. The whole house was vibrating. It felt like a fire truck was parked in the living room. Sneg went around the house checking rooms and peering through the window curtains. Outside he saw a white, near full moon, peppered with grey, shining its light on the sleeping world. The moon lay low on the horizon, casting long shadows of trees and electric poles. In the backyard, a Hills hoist, laden with clothes, swirled in the wind.

Sneg saw baby clothes drying. There were onesies, tops, bibs, pants, and tiny socks. The clothes cast shadows, creating a demon dance on the grass. He shook his head and rubbed his hands across his face.

Maurice stopped howling and took Sneg's pyjama sleeve in his jaws and dragged him to the phone in the hallway. The dog nudged the receiver with his muzzle and howled again. It was late to call the agency, but Sneg didn't think that's what Maurice had in mind. The dog's eyes looked troubled, his howling urgent. Something, Sneg felt, had come up. Something always comes up.

Sneg went to his study and found the papers from the agency. Maurice's owner's name was Rosa Linden. He got the phone book and flipped the pages to 'Hospitals'.

'Are you a family member?' a female voice asked Sneg moments later.

'I'm calling on behalf of one,' Sneg answered, looking at the dog's pleading eyes.

When he was finally put through, it was Rosa's son who picked up the phone. Sneg told him about Maurice, the barking and the howling.

'Maurice,' the son said, 'Maurice is a great dog.' His voice was distant. The phone call was a mistake, Sneg thought. What was he thinking?

'My mother died half an hour ago,' Rosa's son said. 'They were inseparable.'

Sneg offered his condolences and apologised. He said goodbye. And then the son spoke.

'Could you bring Maurice to the hospital? I'll arrange it with the staff.'

'Sure,' Sneg said.

'He needs to know my mother is dead, or he won't stop mourning.'

'We'll be there shortly,' Sneg said.

Rosa's son waited for Sneg and Maurice in front the morgue, a room the size of a walk-in refrigerator, hidden in the bowels of the hospital.

'We have five minutes,' he said to Sneg and a man in blue coveralls next to him nodded and opened the door.

Maurice ran in, propped himself up on the gurney, and sniffed his owner's dead body. The dog pushed her hand with his nose. He understood what had happened, and it hit him hard. He looked at the two men and Rosa's son said, 'She's gone, mate, she's gone.'

Sneg looked at Rosa's body, too. She was small and wrinkled and her face looked like a squeezed lemon. There was no juice left in Rosa.

They were quickly ushered out, and Rosa's son stuffed something into the pocket of the man who opened the door. They sat on the chairs in front of the door.

'You've got to go from something sometime,' Rosa's son said to Sneg while they watched Maurice mourn on the floor. He lay down next to the door with his head between his front legs and cried.

'It was her heart. It just gave out. She stayed asleep after the surgery.' Rosa's son sat next to Sneg and looked blankly at the grey and white chequered floor while he talked. His lips were cracked and his eyes red. He had cried all his tears. The grief will come to collect its dues later, Sneg thought, after the business of the funeral is done. It always does.

'Could you keep him for a little while longer?' Rosa's son pointed at Maurice. 'Please. Until the funeral is done.'

Sneg nodded.

'I'm not sure what to do with him,' Rosa's son said under breath to himself.

Sneg touched the man's shoulder briefly. He didn't know what to say. How do you say to a stranger they are lucky in a moment like that?

On the seventh day since the hospital visit, Maurice finally had a few licks of water. The vet — who Sneg arranged to come for a visit — said the dog was grieving. The young doctor spoke about the range of canine emotions and the importance of acknowledging them.

'He might be like this for the rest of his days. Some pets never recover.'

Sneg never expected to see himself in an animal, but there he was, looking at Maurice and it was like looking into a mirror.

'What can I do?' Sneg asked.

'Hard to say. It varies from dog to dog and from breed to breed. German Shepherds need to know they're useful. They're working dogs. He needs a purpose.'

<hr>

When Sneg thought of the phone conversation, the coldness of the voice still chilled his skin. One has to develop a certain level of emotional detachment working in pounds and kennels, this he knew.

'I'm calling from the Lost Dogs Home in North Melbourne,' the cold voice spoke in an official tone. For a moment, he thought he was listening to a pre-recorded message.

The Home received instructions from the family. Maurice would be taken to the Home, the voice said. The family cannot take care of him right now. It is a difficult time for them. The Home will take care of the dog and do their best to re-house him. They can't promise anything. Maurice is an old dog, but their adoption rate is the highest in the state. They will send someone tomorrow to get the dog, the voice recited.

'That won't be necessary,' Sneg said.

He received the adoption papers two days later. The same day, he called the agency and resigned.

'You'll be missed,' said Agency-man, his voice heavy as always, and thanked him.

<hr>

Maurice watched as Sneg took the Polaroids from the wall. All had dates on the back and he placed them in order in the folder. He then took out the little furniture he had in the room, vacuumed the floor, cleaned the windows and the walls, and mopped the floor.

'This will be your room now. Do you like it?'

Maurice walked into the empty room. Sneg gave him a biscuit and, to his satisfaction, Maurice ate it. The room had a large window that stretched nearly to the floor and gave out onto the street.

'Here,' Sneg pointed at the bottom of the window, 'here, I'm going to make a bench. So you can lay and watch the world go by. Get some sunshine.'

Maurice sniffed the area in question and sat.

'Don't worry, I've got all the tools,' Sneg said, more to himself. 'The knowledge is still up here.' He touched his head. 'I can do it, no worries,' he reassured himself, went to the shed and got his tools.

'Time to do some shopping. Are you coming?' he called Maurice.

In the hardware store, Sneg bought some timber, screws, nails, brackets and glue. In the corner of the store, he saw doghouses for sale. He went back and got more timber.

Two days later Maurice's house started taking shape and Sneg noticed a smidgen of excitement in his eyes. Or maybe it was just the light reflecting in his pupils. Sneg looked at his handiwork.

'Not bad,' he said as he drilled a pilot hole for the screw.

Sneg and Maurice waited for the groundskeeper to open the cemetery gate.

'Good morning,' the groundskeeper greeted them. 'With a friend today?'

'Maurice, say hello,' Sneg said, but Maurice remained quiet. His tail was tucked and he averted his gaze.

'You latest assignment is not very talkative,' the groundskeeper said.

'He's mine now. We came to visit his old owner.' Sneg handed over a piece of paper with Rosa's name on it. The groundskeeper nodded and pointed out where the grave was.

'First Rosa and then I'll take you to meet my boy,' Sneg said to Maurice and pulled out two photos from inside his jacket. Maurice whined and then barked once when he recognised Rosa.

'Rosa is with him now.' Sneg put the photos together and Maurice sniffed them. 'He's been here for a very long time. He'll take care of her.'

'We'll stay awhile, I think,' Sneg said to the groundskeeper.

Sneg and Maurice drove to the pet store. It was time to restock. In front of the entrance Sneg tied Maurice to a post and the dog slumped on the concrete, uninterested. Inside, the girl, Alicia, stood behind the computer screen. Opposite her was a young man stabbing his index finger on the counter. Sneg came closer and saw the girl was crying. Black tears ran down her cheeks. The young man gave Sneg a once over and continued with his blast. In between rants, he puffed nervously on a cigarette.

Sneg asked Alicia if everything was all right. She shook her head. The young man approached Sneg, took a puff, dropped the cigarette, and stubbed it out with his foot. He blew smoke in Sneg's face and told him to stay out of it.

Sneg opened his mouth to say something but the young man shoved him with both hands in his chest and he fell down, knocking over neatly stacked birdcages behind him. Alicia screamed at him to stop and he screamed back at her to shut up. Sneg tried to gather himself on his knees and then he saw a black mass rapidly enter the store.

It was Maurice.

Some two meters away from his target, Maurice leaped. This time, he didn't break his flight. He landed on the young man's chest with all his might and anger and knocked him down. The young man lifted his arms toward his face. Maurice didn't bark or bite. He opened his jaws and put his fangs on the young man's neck. His petrified face disappeared behind the dog's head.

A low growl came out of the Maurice's throat. He lifted his gaze toward his new master and Sneg crawled to him. He grabbed his collar and spoke to him calmly.

'It's all right boy. It's all right. I'm all right. You did well. You did real well. You can let go now.'

Maurice looked into Sneg's eyes, making sure this is what his new master wanted.

'Let go Maurice, *let go*.' And Maurice let go.

Sneg ordered the young man to leave, and he promptly did, stumbling a couple of times before finally finding the exit. Sneg looked at Maurice's leash and saw it was cut clean.

Alicia came and knelt down next to them. She wasn't crying anymore. She looked relieved.

'Maurice, this is Alicia,' Sneg said. The girl threw herself at the dog and hugged him. She then hugged Sneg and gave him a kiss on the cheek, before she went back to Maurice. She took the dog's face into her hands and kissed him, rubbing his neck and under his chin.

'You're such a good boy Maurice,' she said. 'Such a good boy.'

Maurice barked, wagged his tail and licked her face.

MUSCLES AND NERVE

I have nothing planned for the evening, so when my boss asks if I want to stay back and do some overtime, I let him squirm for a bit before saying yes. Everyone in the store turned down his offer. I'm the last employee he approaches. Someone has to stay back and serve our regular customer, Klaus, a wedding photographer.

My boss, Klaus and the sales lady Wendy have a longstanding arrangement. Klaus comes every Friday afternoon around five twenty, just before the shop closes, and buys a truckload of film. He buys 35 mm and medium format rolls, black and white and colour, negative and transparency. Klaus spends a lot and the boss makes sure he's happy. Wendy stays back for this sale and she closes the store afterwards. She keeps the commission and gets paid for one-hour double time.

Wendy is thirty something, blonde and a real looker and my boss thinks this is what makes Klaus come back to us. I've had dealings with Klaus and I know the only thing that makes him happy is the price. He also likes men. Wendy never told our boss this, as she needs the commission, the overtime and the tip.

Sometimes, Klaus comes after we are closed, and Wendy stays and waits for him. Today Klaus calls and says he will be coming around eight in the evening. Wendy tells our boss to find someone else to serve Klaus. She says she can't stay late even if she got paid triple time.

Wendy has two children and a husband. Everyone knows Wendy has some problems with her husband. We workers get together and talk crap about whoever isn't with us at the moment. We're worse than a sewing circle. I make a point of knowing as much as I can about everyone, including the regular customers. You never know when you might have to use a certain piece of information as leverage.

Wendy's husband is a classic dropkick. Drinks, gambles, and whores around. One morning I was helping Wendy set up the cameras in the store window before we opened and she started sobbing. I didn't say anything. She pulled out a child's drawing. She told me it was her daughter's. In it the girl drew herself, her brother and Wendy. There was no father in the picture.

It's so sad, Wendy said, rubbing her red eyes. My husband worked like a maniac to make a home for us and I never said anything. He never did anything for himself. It's my fault too.

I didn't like seeing Wendy cry.

I watch my boss go from one employee to another. No one can or wants to stay and work late. Some give him lame excuses, some flat out decline. My boss sighs and walks toward me. I have no one waiting for me in my flat. Not even a pet that needs to be fed.

My boss talks about how my recent work performance has improved and I deserve more responsibility. He asks if I would like to close the store tonight. While he waffles, I remember my last performance review and how in the general comments section, he wrote *ample room for improvement in all facets of the business*. He doesn't look like a guy who'd know what facet means. He was mildly surprised when I signed the review without any protest.

So when he asks me what I think of his offer, I tell him I'm thinking of going to the Russell Street cinema to watch a movie. There's this movie about a serial killer whose murders mimic the seven deadly sins. I know I'm never going to watch it. I hear there's a fair bit of blood in the movie. I don't mind ghosts and aliens, but a drop of blood on the screen and I have nightmares for a week. I also tell my boss there's a footy game on later and I might watch the game. Everyone knows I don't follow sports. Then my boss pulls twenty dollars out of his wallet and stuffs it in my hand. He says it's my dinner money and I can use the darkroom. My boss is a smart man, that's why he's the boss. He makes me an offer I can't refuse.

There's a rumour circling in the store he's a die-hard fan of *Dr Phil*. He records the day's episode and watches it at night. He reckons this gives him better insight into his employees. It's like some psychology course he's taking by studying this famous TV doctor.

I work as a casual part-timer, Wednesday to Saturday, from ten to three, covering the busiest part of the day in the commercial section of the store, where the high-end SLR cameras are. The only reason I work in a photographic store is because of the discount on film and printing paper.

I agree to stay back on Friday night. The lure of my own darkroom is too much. I plan to finish my assignments in portraiture and develop half a dozen rolls of black and white film before printing. I'm studying photography part-time at TAFE in Collingwood. We get darkroom time allocated in school, but it's always an arm wrestle to get a good enlarger and a sharp lens. I prefer being alone in the store after hours.

My boss and I shake hands on our deal and he tells me to talk to Wendy. I know everything Wendy tells me about Klaus, but I listen anyway. I could listen to Wendy all day. Klaus can be a bit finicky. He doesn't like buying film that wasn't stored in the fridge and has a short expiry date. Other than that, he's a great tipper.

I like Wendy. I often think about her. This was a little weird in the beginning, as she knows my mum and she's only a few years younger than her. Wendy's the reason I got the job. She's in the same book club as my mum. A bunch of ladies meet every Wednesday night for tea and scones in the Deer Park library. Sometimes they talk about books. When I started, Wendy helped me get the lay of the land. She showed me things. Like how to sell extra camera accessories and increase your commission. Most people don't know this, but sales margins are much higher on camera bags and filters than on the actual camera. And Wendy knew all the tricks.

Last Christmas we took a group photo and Wendy stood next to me. Her boob touched my arm. It was a hot day and everyone was in the short-sleeve uniform and I could feel her nipple on my skin. Since then I've had a thing for Wendy. I cut out the two of us so I could wank. It was weird with me in the photo, so in the end there was only Wendy.

Wendy tells me as soon as she closes up, a homeless man called Pete comes and parks himself in the recessed entrance of the store. She says he's polite and harmless. Pete's the guy who sells the *Big Issue* on the street. I strain my brain, but I can't picture him. I've seen a homeless guy carrying papers in his backpack, but he's always blended into the streetscape, like a bench or a lamppost.

At three o'clock, I finish my shift and walk out of the store. I have two hours to kill and I'm hungry. I go into this little Thai place on Elizabeth Street and order green chicken curry.

I say number one, takeaway, please. The woman behind the counter, not lifting her eyes from her magazine, says ten minutes, ten dollars.

It takes ten seconds to slap a ladle of pre-cooked curry on a serving of pre-cooked rice, but they always say ten minutes. As though they're cooking it from scratch. Even the pizza place is the same. They pre-prepare the dough and toppings and it takes them two minutes to cook a pizza in the wood-fired oven.

The place isn't busy. There are two older guys near the window playing a board game. They push little wooden pieces like they're commanding armies on the battlefield. I sit next to the window and stare out. People are looking upward, checking the darkening afternoon sky loaded with rain clouds. I look at the street again. That's when I see the fox.

The fox is in a cage being carried by a man in a dark green uniform and akubra hat. The man walks further down the street and sits on the bench in front of the General Post Office on Bourke Street. He puts the cage next to his feet and pulls out a bottle of water from his pants side pocket.

I grab my food, leave ten bucks on the counter, and run to him. I find out the fox was caught in Flagstaff Gardens, a large park on the edge of the city. The ranger says it is probably an urban fox that came from the western suburbs travelling along the Maribyrnong River, using bushland along the bicycle tracks and walking paths as cover, then making a left turn at Dynon Road.

It probably raided chicken coops along the way and snatched the odd pet rabbit, he says. He takes off his hat and puts it on his knee. He wipes his bald head with his shirtsleeve. The oily scalp leaves a wet patch on his shirt. I see some fresh scratches on his hands. It must be from handling the fox.

I tell him I had no idea there were such things as urban foxes.

Yeah, they're mostly in outer suburbs, he says, but every so often, one or two more daring ones venture closer to the city.

You see how the fur is not as red as your regular fox? It's like they're adapting to the greyness of the city streets.

I nod, but I have no idea about the real red colour of a fox's fur. Just like he has no idea about correct exposure and film speeds.

I look at the fox curled up into a ball on one side of the cage. Wide eyes are peering over its front legs.

Is it a boy or a girl? I ask.

A girl and she's pregnant.

Where are you going to release her?

We're not. She's going to be put down. Foxes are pests.

They are?

Yep, my theory is she came to the city because right now there's baiting going on in the country. The government is trying to reduce the population. They're also after rabbits.

I stick my finger through the cage mesh and the fox snaps her jaws.

She looks like a plucky one, I say.

She is, but she's also scared. It took some guts to travel this far.

Why did she?

Looking for a place to deliver her babies, I reckon. City parks are full of birds, mice, human food scraps. Easy, quick meals for her.

The ranger looks at me eating. That curry any good? I'm starving.

I nod, give him a thumbs-up and point at the Thai place.

I return to the store and after everyone leaves, I retreat to the darkroom while I wait for Klaus. After I develop my rolls, I put them into the drying cabinet. I walk to the front of the store and see Pete, the homeless guy, lying outside in the doorway, reading a newspaper. It's a little after six. I'm doing well with time.

The first frame I print is a photo of my grandfather. He's an old man living in an old person's home, waiting to die. When I photographed him, I took him outside into the garden and sat him against the plain white wall. I shot him in the open shade, no lights, no reflectors, slow speed, fine grain, black and white film, to capture every detail of his weathered face. It's mostly alcohol and cigarettes that did the damage and an occasional beating he received in his younger days, I'm sure.

My grandfather wasn't really in the mood, so I had to bribe him with some booze, which I put in a juice bottle. He wasn't getting relaxed, so I got him talking about his days as a crook. He didn't like being called a crook and yelled at me, but he opened up.

He told me he was in Long Bay Gaol, up in Sydney, at the same time as the infamous bank robber Darcy Dugan. My grandfather was inside on a six-month sentence for stealing a motorcycle on a dare. He said he never had trouble with the law after that. This I know was the truth. He left Sydney, never to return, and spent the rest of his years in a factory in Altona where they made buckets and basins and such.

He said Dugan approached him, and a few other Irishmen, to help him escape. I'm Irish on my father's side. Dugan paid them with cigarettes. All they had to do was create a diversion by rioting and fighting amongst themselves. Someone suggested starting a fire but Dugan scolded the man.

Dugan was a decent crook, my grandfather said. A real, old-fashioned crook for life. He spent half his life in prison and the way he did things was simple. Not much planning went into his robberies. It was all muscles and nerve. Like the time he and one of his mates walked into a fine art auction and took some expensive painting right off the easel. Then they boxed their way out.

I finish my proofs and look through the loupe, trying to pick which frame to print first. I catch sight of my wristwatch. It's well after eight. Klaus is a no-show. Could it be I didn't hear him? I'm a little angry. I didn't care much about losing the sale but was hoping to have a chat with Klaus about my work. Get a professional opinion. Klaus made a name for himself when he was younger, exhibiting his prints around Melbourne.

I step into the store to get out of the chemical-filled air in the darkroom. I walk to the front and see Pete in the door. He's sleeping. His back is turned toward the glass, and I see his body rhythmically moving up and down. He produces steam through his nose and it looks like his beanie-covered head is on fire. I return to the darkroom.

I think of Pete as I focus the faces of the people I photographed on the enlarger baseboard. He looks quite young, which means he's younger than he looks. Life on the street must be tough. I hear him cough. I put him out of my mind and start to print.

It's after midnight and I start putting the prints through the wash when I hear a fracas outside. I step into the darkened shop and see moving shadows on the floor. Four men, holding beer bottles in their hands, stand above Pete, who is now sitting. His head is lowered. The men yell at him and one of them prods Pete in the ribs with his foot. After a minute or so, the men stop yelling at Pete and they move away a few paces. They light their cigarettes. I see Pete lifting his hand and putting it to his mouth. He asks them for a cigarette.

This is when they all come back and start kicking Pete. He scrunches into a ball while the blows rain on him. I grab the phone from the counter and call the police. Realising Pete could be dead by the time they arrive, I run to the glass cabinet where the fire extinguisher is.

I'm going to spray the men to create a diversion and drag Pete inside. There's a key for it somewhere in the office but there's no time to look for it. The glass is supposed to be broken in an emergency. If I break the glass I will lose the element of surprise. There's much yelling and screaming. Pete's the one screaming. I wrap my jacket around my elbow and carefully break the glass.

I turn my eyes to the door again. They haven't heard me.

There are shadows of four men dancing on the floor and I step on their shadows, their heads, and their hands as I slowly walk toward the door. I'm holding the extinguisher in one hand and the nozzle in the other, ready to pull the safety pin.

Pete's face is now glued to the shop window. This is the first time I see him properly. He's got a thin face and grey eyes. Maybe they were blue once.

Blood is gushing out of his mouth and his skull. Rivers of blood out of such a skinny man. The next time I sleep, I will have nightmares. I take a few more steps. The men beating Pete can see me now, but they're too busy. They're not lifting their heads. Pete can see me too. But he doesn't call for help.

Blood is everywhere. It's on the concrete, on the glass and even coming under the door and into the shop and getting soaked up by the carpet. Someone's going to have to clean this mess. Someone will have to put on long cleaning gloves and a facemask, just like I do when working in the darkroom.

It's going to be hard yakka cleaning all the mess. There's also the glass I broke. Someone will have to scoop it up. And my prints, they need to be hung to dry.

Pete pulls his backpack over his head. The extinguisher gets heavy in my sweaty hands and I put it on the floor. I wipe my palms on my pants.

COMPLICATION

It's Thursday afternoon and I've come home from work with a termination letter in my hand. I'm at the front door when my wife Meira says, 'The fridge is dead.' Meira is wearing a kitchen apron and has tongs in one hand and a spatula in another. The house smells like cheap hot dogs and fried onions.

'I'm cooking all the meat from the freezer,' she says this as though we keep a lot of frozen meat. The last time I put my face in the freezer I saw half a kilo of beef mince, four chicken breasts and a bag of mixed corn and peas.

When I hear about the fridge, I give a snort in response and bend down to undo the laces on my boots. Meira goes back inside the house and I leave my steel caps on the front porch. I take my lunch leftovers out of my bag and toss them on the grass for the birds. A raven lands on the lawn. It takes a piece of bread crust in its beak and flies off to my neighbour's roof, where it presents this gift to another slightly smaller raven. Ravens, I've heard, pair for life.

In the kitchen, I pull the fridge out from between the wall and the bench until I can see the back of it. I think about my day off, which I always spend sleeping in and watching old cricket matches I taped off the tellie years ago. Then I think of Faruk. Meira knows what I'm thinking, and she says, 'Don't call Faruk.'

In the afternoon before my day off, I often call this young bloke, Faruk, from the end of the street. He works in a warehouse in Laverton and knows a place in Burnside where they make the best *chevapi* in Melbourne. On his way back from work, if I ask him, he'll bring me ten pieces served in *somun* bread with sauerkraut and goat's milk yogurt. For Meira, he brings a potato and onion pita and a small bouquet of flowers. Faruk is into flowers and trees, studying to be a botanist.

'The fridge is dead, not me,' I say to Meira.

'It's the anniversary of his sister's death. Give the boy some space.'

Faruk told me about his sister being shot by a sniper during the siege of Sarajevo and I told him about my brother. How they tied him hand and foot to a pine tree and cut his belly open with precision and purpose, just enough for the bowels to show and bleed. It was winter and the birds and animals were hungry.

I kneel down and peek in behind the large panel that hides the parts that run the fridge. Wires, pipes, condenser and compressor are hiding inside. But I have no idea how to fix it. When I push the fridge back into position, my wife is behind me. I turn to face her and we look at each other for a few moments. I reach for the letter in my front pocket, but Meira shakes her head and says, 'Fridge, tomorrow.' She snaps the kitchen tongs in front of my face and I nod.

From a bowl on the kitchen table I grab a handful of peanuts and shove them in my mouth. I'm almost through crunching the nuts into oblivion when I hear a crack from my right upper molar. I wince and my right eye twitches closed. I grab for the paper towel and spit the peanut mash out. Meira, enveloped in steam and smoke, doesn't turn around from the stove. Salt coats my tongue and I run my index finger across my teeth. I reach my second-last molar and feel its rough surface. Then I carefully poke the peanut mash on the bench until I find the missing part of my tooth. It's a fair-sized chunk.

I go to the hallway and stand in front of the mirror, which is not quite body length. Every time I look in that mirror, I regret buying it. It's useless. I can never see myself fully. My feet are always missing and if I step backwards, I hit the wall of the hallway. If I come closer in to see my feet, they look too small for my body, distorted by looking down from above.

I'm about to open my mouth and try to get a look at the broken tooth when I notice something is different at the end of the hallway. I walk over and see three framed pictures on the wall that were not there yesterday. Two of the photographs show Meira's parents. Her father as a young soldier is in one, her mother as a little girl in the other. The third photo is of my maternal grandmother. An angry face looking off into the distance, draped in a *shamija*, a kind of colourful headdress. They're the only pictures Meira and I managed to save before our village was torched.

'I can't have my grandmother on the wall next to your parents,' I call out to Meira and she comes into the hallway. 'She's evil,' I continue. 'You know that. She could drive a wedge between these two wall pictures.' Meira dismisses me with a curt wave of her hand.

When I was five, I had a pet rooster. We were born on the same day. His name was Beli. My grandmother hated the way Beli came to me to be petted and that I fed him the best food I could scrounge. He loved boiled corn. She said I was spoiling him and that I needed to learn that these were farm animals, not pets. She killed my pet rooster by cutting his head off with an axe on a stump. Then she made me eat him. I cried for months until I developed cysts on my eye. And I mean on my eyes, not my eyelids. You get these clear pimple-like things on your eyes. I still have tiny scars on my pupils that look like pencilled dots.

In the kitchen I say, 'I'd give two years of my life if I could give her a piece of my mind.'

'Be careful with your wishes. Remember Omer Salčin?' Meira says.

'Yes, I do.'

Omer Salčin was our neighbour who said he'd give two years of his life for his wife to give him a son after she gave him four daughters. When his wife gave him the fifth baby, a son, Omer Salčin, died the next day. The whole *mahala* said that if he hadn't died, he would've lived only two more years.

I inspect my damaged tooth in the mirror. I see the dark-grey exposed filling. I can't remember exactly how old it is, but it was there before we came to Melbourne. Which means before the war started. I had no dental work done during the war, no-one did. You were lucky if they patched you up after you were shot. Even if you were lucky and were only hit by shrapnel, there was always the dreaded infection. What bombs and bullets didn't finish, infection did. Infection was like an old and thorough cleaner, diligently mopping every corner.

I go back to the living room, sit on the sofa and turn on the tellie. The voice coming from the box talks about watch-making. Some very expensive handmade watches have extremely intricate functions. The camera zooms into the back of the watch and long, old fingers lift the cover. The voice says the watch has a calendar, an alarm and a simple chronograph, and goes on to explain that some watches can show moon phases and others that even have a planetarium dial. Some have a mechanical refinement called *tourbillon*, which lessens the effect of gravity on the operation of the timepiece. The more elaborate the watch, the more parts it requires. Some timepieces have more than a thousand moving parts. A feature on a watch that goes beyond a simple display of hours and minutes is called a complication. The more of them a watch has, the more valuable it is.

My forehead creases, thinking about all those little barrels, springs, wheels, and pinions moving. Sweat beads on my temples. My tooth begins to throb. From the kitchen pantry, I fish out a bottle of *rakija*. I take a swig and swirl the homemade plum brandy around my broken tooth. When the *rakija* loses its bite, I swallow it and then I take another long swig. This time I don't swirl, I just drink. Strong liquor dulls the pain fast. Now there's just the discomfort of the ragged edge of the tooth rubbing on my gums and tongue. In the hallway next to the telephone, I flip through a book filled with business cards. When I find the dentist's number, I quickly dial but I get a recorded message. I look at my wristwatch, which has just the three hands and no complications. It's after 5 pm.

When Meira finishes cooking, she applies a cream to her hands and arms. She works in a continental deli on the slicing machine, cutting cheeses and cold meats. A week ago she was put in the seafood section, because the fish guy went on holiday, and since then she'd come home cranky. Her hands and arms are covered in red itchy blotches. She reckons she's allergic to fish, but hasn't been to see a doctor. Wearing gloves doesn't help her. I tell her to talk to the boss but she says that she'll manage for one more week.

I work in a recycling factory with a dozen other blokes, sorting out plastic and glass bottles, paper and cans. Today, in anticipation of my day off, I slowed down my pace. The conveyor belt had to be stopped a few times so that the work I had missed could be finished. I went to the toilet a couple of times and stayed there for fifteen minutes. After my second visit, my supervisor put me on the sucker, the large suction tube at the end of the conveyor, which sucks the rubbish not sorted out by busy workers' hands. All you have to do is pick up an occasional can or glass bottle that has been missed. There's a chair and a bunch of magazines next to the sucker.

At lunchtime, our boss came to the lunchroom and said he had an announcement. He looked at his clipboard when he said this. His neck was red, just like the day I found him in the paper pit. On that day I had returned to work to pick up my lunchbox, which I had forgotten. The factory gate was still open but I couldn't see anyone. I grabbed my box, then I heard someone outside swear. I went around the building to where the four pits are: one each for cans, glass, plastic and paper. In the paper pit, I found my boss, the owner of the joint, sleeves rolled up, waist deep in paper and cardboard. He held a stack of pornographic magazines in his hands, which he had fished out. When he looked up and saw me, I lifted my lunchbox in the air and he nodded.

So this same guy gathered his workers to tell them he was closing down the recycling factory for a month. He said he was bringing in new equipment and machinery, that it was time to drag the place into the twenty-first century and make sure health and safety regulations were followed. There would be some new magnets, conveyer belts, moving separators, and a huge suction tube at the end. He called the sucker a suction tube. To me it sounded as though everything would be same before as before, but newer. He said he wished everyone all the best, and he hoped they had a good time during the break.

When the shift ended, I found an envelope tucked into the ventilation slit of my locker door. I looked around the locker room and all but four lockers had envelopes. The letter said that due to restructuring of the operations, the number of employees needed would be scaled down. There were bullet-point instructions about where to leave my work uniform and safety boots, and it explained that my last pay, together with the rest of my entitlements, would be deposited into my bank account on Monday. There weren't any figures given, nothing that detailed what I was owed. As the workers read their letters they started swearing and slamming their locker doors. Before things could boil over, half a dozen security guards came and escorted us sacked workers to the car park.

Now Meira comes into the living room. Her hands and elbows are covered in cream and she's holding them up in the air.

'I'm chucking a sickie tomorrow,' she says.

'Good,' I say.

'We can buy a fridge tomorrow.'

I pull up my upper lip, show her the cracked tooth, and tell her what happened.

'Do we have any painkillers?' I ask her.

'I'll have a look,' Meira says.

'No, let that cream soak in. Tell me where to look. Bathroom cupboard or breadbasket on the microwave?'

'Try the breadbasket.'

I find two Panadeine Forte and swallow them with *rakija*.

Back in the living room, I tell Meira about what happened at work today. She opens her mouth to respond, but I hear a noise and interrupt her before she can get the words out.

'Did you hear that?' I ask, relieved to change the topic. 'Something's scratching at the front door.'

'It's Mitzi. Bring her in.'

'Mitzi?'

'The neighbour's cat that I've been feeding. They moved out and left her. She's ours now.'

I start for the front door.

'Reuf, be careful if you pick her up. She's pregnant,' Meira says. 'The vet said they can spay her and do the abortion for about $300.'

'We're not keeping the kittens?'

'What are we going to do with kittens? God knows there are plenty of cats on this earth.'

I open the door for Mitzi and she lets out a small chirrup and then parks herself on the welcome mat. I bend over and pat her, and she rubs her face on my hand but doesn't move. This is what cats do. They'll wake you up in the middle of the night to get inside and then take their time to cross the threshold.

'She's not coming in,' I yell out to Meira, 'I'm picking her up.'

'Gently,' she yells back, but when I look at the spot where the cat was, it is empty. I turn around and look down the hallway and see the cat's tail disappear into the kitchen. Meira brings two bowls, food and water, and puts them in the hallway and the cat starts eating.

'She looks like Prince,' I say.

'Like Prince?'

'Yeah, remember Prince? The butcher's tomcat.'

'Prince was orange and stripy and fluffy,' Meira says.

Twenty years ago, when we came to Melbourne, Meira and I lived in a flat above the butcher's shop. I picture Prince and I see a black and white cat running up the stairs to our entrance door.

'I'll sleep on the sofa tonight,' I say. 'Between your hands and my tooth, we won't get much sleep together.'

'We'll figure out about the job, don't worry,' she says and I nod.

In the dead of night, I leap like a salmon out of a restless sleep. The right side of my face is throbbing. I take two Panadol with a swig from the *rakija* bottle. Everything is quiet except for a rustling in the backyard. I sneak into the bedroom and get the torch from Meira's bedside table. She's sleeping with clenched fists, her hands close to her body.

In the backyard, I look at the sky. Over the roofs of houses and through the leaves of gums, a new day is breaking. I hear low, rasping croaks. I shine the torch across the yard and see black feathers. It's a raven, as black as the inside of a buried coffin. Something is wrong with it, it's hopping around in distress, trying to flap its wings and fly away.

I check the time on my wristwatch. It's four o'clock. The hand marking seconds moves at the same pace as the throbbing in my tooth.

I pick the raven up carefully and take it into the shed, where I see a wing is broken and bloody. I put it on the floor and sit on a garden chair. The bird lifts its head and looks me in the eyes, and then its head falls back to the concrete.

Lost job, broken fridge, cracked tooth, pregnant cat, injured raven. The more complications a watch has, the more valuable it is.

From my toolbox, I find the pliers. With my left hand, I splash *rakija* over the jaws of the pliers. I open my mouth wide and grip my upper lip, pulling it up to my nostrils. The jaws of the pliers are fixed around my tooth when I hear tapping on the shed door.

I release my upper lip and put the pliers down. When I open the door, another raven is standing at the threshold, spreading its black wings and croaking. I stumble backwards, but catch myself on the doorframe. This raven is bigger than the injured one. A male. He slowly walks in and approaches the body of his mate. He nudges her head with his beak but she doesn't move.

He begins dragging the dead bird back towards the door and out onto the grass. He stalks around the body, shrieking once, twice, three times. The raven stands above his dead mate for some time, then flies off and lands on my neighbour's roof.

I stick the pliers back in my mouth, take a firm grip and yank hard. Blood fills my mouth.

I take the shovel from the rack on the shed wall and push the blade into the ground next to the dead raven. I start digging. The raven on the roof flaps his wings, drops his head down and lets out a deep, gurgling call.

About the author

Fikret Pajalic came to Melbourne as a refugee, learnt English in his mid-twenties and started writing years later. He has won and placed in competitions, published in anthologies and literary magazines. His fiction has appeared in *Meanjin, Overland, Westerly, Etchings, Sleepers, Antipodes, The Big Issue, Hotel Amerika, Wisconsin Review, The Minnesota Review, Fjords Review, Sheepshead Review, Bop Dead City, Structo, Paper and Ink, JAAM* and elsewhere. For a full list of his publication achievements and to read samples of his work view his Literary CV. In 2014 he was awarded a Creative Victoria grant, and in 2015 an Australia Council grant for the development of his literary manuscript '*Wanderings*' and in 2016 from Brimbank City Council for the development of chapbook . He is married to author Amra Pajalic and they live in Melbourne's western suburbs with their daughter.

CONNECT WITH FIKRET

https://www.fikretpajalic.com/

 instagram.com/fikretpajalic17/

CONNECT WITH PISHUKIN PRESS

 facebook.com/PishukinPress

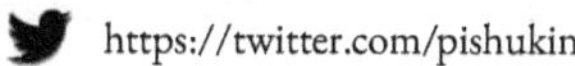 https://twitter.com/pishukin

Publication Credits

Boonie, *Overland*, Issue 215, June 2014

The Flock, *JAAM Literary Journal* (NZ), Issue 31, October 2013

Tomorrow, *Southerly*, Issue 75.3, Spring 2016

Mahala, *The Minnesota Review* (USA), Issue 85, Nov 2015

Mahala, *Grapple Annual*, Issue 2, Nov 2015

Names of Wildflowers, chapbook (Brimbank Council Grant), September 2016

Names of Wildflowers, *The Florida Review*, Issue 40/2, Autumn 2016

Soul to Sell - Shortlisted in *Overland NUW Fair Australia Prize 2015*, June 2015

Incision - Shortlisted in *Ada Cambridge Short Story Prize 2014*, May 2014

Wasps, *Fjords Review* (USA), Fall Issue, November 2014

Wasps, *21D Magazine*, October 2014

Wasps, *The Victorian Writer*, November Issue, 2015

Dinosaur, *Westerly Magazine*, Vol.58, No.2, November 2013

Complication, *Best Summer Stories*, Black Inc, Summer 2018

Complication, *Hotel Amerika*, Issue 14, Spring 2017

Complication, *Meanjin*, Autumn Issue, Vol 74, No 1, March 2015

'If you struggle to read, then you haven't found the right book format.'

I'm Amra Pajalić, the owner and publisher of Pishukin Press, an independent press dedicated to the publication of under-represented writers of fiction and nonfiction, as well as genre fiction.

There is a quote that states 'If you don't like to read, then you haven't found the right book.' I would like to extend that further and state that 'If you struggle to read then you haven't found the right book format.' As a high school teacher I have taught students with various individual needs and recognise the need to make books accessible for all kinds of readers. To this end I am committed to publishing all Pishukin Press titles in as many formats as possible. This includes:

Dyslexic Format Edition—printed in Dyslexic Open font in 14 point
Large Print edition—printed in Large Print Open Sans No Italics font in 18 point font size
Audiobooks AI—narrated by artificial intelligence using Google technology.
Audiobooks—narrated by performance narrators.
All books are also available in paperback and hardcover editions.

To get 10% off use discount code 10OFF

https://www.pishukinpress.com/